BACKSHOOTER

Reece Willard and Dandy Sam Foley were partners running the Rolling Dice Saloon in Three Forks, Montana. When they took out an extra loan for an adjoining dance hall, neither had any idea that the crooked bank manager would trick them. Threatened with eviction, the partners were forced to take the law into their own hands. But Reece served time in the state penitentiary for it, whilst the treacherous Sam escaped justice. Now released from prison, Reece is hot on Sam's trail — will he get his revenge?

DALE GRAHAM

BACKSHOOTER

Complete and Unabridged

LINFORD
Leicester

First published in Great Britain in 2013 by
Robert Hale Limited
London

First Linford Edition
published 2015
by arrangement with
Robert Hale Limited
London

A catalogue record for this book is available
from the British Library.

ISBN 978–1–4448–2465–0

Published by
F. A. Thorpe (Publishing)
Anstey, Leicestershire

Set by Words & Graphics Ltd.
Anstey, Leicestershire
Printed and bound in Great Britain by
T. J. International Ltd., Padstow, Cornwall

This book is printed on acid-free paper

1

Release

'Do your duty, Mr Crow!'

The gruff tones of the governor echoed around the starkly bare stone walls of Butte Hill Centre of Correction, Montana's infamous penitentiary.

The grim name was a play on words that was always exercised by the governor when welcoming new inmates. 'We have one of our very own outside the prison walls,' he would jovially regale the greenhorn convicts. 'And there's always a place reserved for those who want to cause trouble.'

It soon became obvious to all newcomers that Butte Hill was no holiday camp. And the governor made sure that convicts who bucked the system were dealt with in a severe manner.

Such a prisoner was now awaiting his punishment in the open yard below.

'And make sure to lay it on with a will,' ordered Governor Wallace Glasgow. Obediah Crow was the guard assigned to carry out the brutal chastizement of prisoner 6715. Reece Willard was strapped to a wooden frame in the centre of the prison courtyard. Overhead a burning midday sun beat down with relentless fury turning the yard into a simmering cauldron.

Slowly the guard approached the tethered prisoner. Shaking out the deadly cat o' nine tails, he stuck a lump of leather between Willard's teeth.

'Bite down hard on this,' he whispered ostensibly checking that the fastenings were secure. 'And remember that it ain't me that's giving you this whipping.'

'Just get on with it, Crow,' Willard replied, trying to suppress the nervous inflection in his voice.

Even though he had never previously

experienced a flogging, its effects were starkly etched in his mind. He had seen at first hand the ragged network of scars left behind. A bestial lifetime's reminder of a convict's sojourn in Butte Hill. More than one who felt the lick of the cat were now residing permanently in the prison cemetery.

Warder Crow had shown a sympathetic leaning towards prisoner 6715. The two unlikely associates had formed a tentative respect for one another. Nothing too obvious was revealed that could draw any noteworthy attention to his partiality and so lead to charges of favouritism. Just the odd easier job now and again. Also, extra rations when the recalcitrant convict had found himself thrust into the prison's notorious punishment facility known as the Hole.

And where Reece Willard was concerned, those visits had been decidedly above the average. As a result, he had acquired the nickname of the Mule — though not on account of his large ears that stuck out like batwings, nor his unkempt mass of greasy black hair.

By displaying a stubborn streak of orneriness, he had earned the wrath of Butte's irascible governor.

Nobody was allowed to show any spirit in Wallace Glasgow's institution. Those that balked at towing the line invited the full measure of his choleric displeasure. In such places, the governor was all-powerful. This indisputable purveyor of discipline and justice was judge, jury and even executioner should that be warranted.

The Mule, more than most, had earned that disapprobation throughout the seven years of his incarceration.

Even on the day before his release, he had refused an order to be strip-searched. This had been given under the trumped-up charge that he had stolen tobacco from the prison shop. A fight had ensued. And four guards had been needed to subdue him.

Glasgow could have added a further six months to his sentence but he had decided to make an example of the fractious convict by awarding him a dozen strokes of the cat. It was a display of the sadistic streak the governor relished. A public flogging was reserved for special occasions.

Willard's offence on his last day was judged to be one of those.

'So what are you waiting for, Mr Crow?' snapped Glasgow, from the raised balcony where he was reclining on a couch like an emperor of ancient Rome waiting to enjoy a gladiatorial contest. A cigar in one hand and a glass of finest French brandy in the other, he took a delicate sip before adding, 'We're all waiting to enjoy the entertainment.'

The leery smile creasing the brute's owlish features brought a flurry of hoots and whistles from the assembled convicts locked away in their cells. Many of the barred windows over-looked the courtyard. From these a host of lurid comments poured forth.

'Don't let the bastard crush your

spirit, Mule,' called out one hidden voice.

'You'll get your'n one day, Glasgow,' howled another rabid patron.

'And we'll all be there cheering you into hell,' from another.

The governor issued a blunt order to the head warder on his left. Seconds later, a rattling fusilade of gunfire echoed around the yard as the Gatling gun opened up. Bullets scythed across the stone walls driving the watching convicts down on to the floors of their cells.

When the ear-shattering burst had died away, an ominous silence descended over the prison enclave.

'Punishment will be carried out forthwith,' rasped the governor who had known for some time the favour being shown to prisoner 6715. That was the reason he had selected Crow to carry it out.

The first blow thudded against the Mule's back. The dull sound elicited a sharp intake of breath from those

6

forced to listen and take heed. The tails were shaken out before the next blow rained down.

And so it continued.

Each stoke of the lash drew more blood, leaving lacerated strips of flesh hanging from the scourged torso. And through it all not a sound emerged from Willard's tightly clamped jaws. The victim stoically refused to acknowledge the brutal punishment. All that anyone watching could detect was a slight arching of the back as the muscles tensed to receive the harsh beating.

After what to everybody watching and listening seemed like a lifetime, the torture was finally over. Willard then spat out the shreds of leather that had been bitten clean through.

Only then did he cry out when his back was doused with a bucket of salted water. This was the traditional method of supposedly cauterizing the wounds and thus preventing the spread of infection. In truth, it was a final act of brutality to hector the victim.

Hence the saying to rub salt in the wounds.

A pregnant silence followed. Only the harshly grating rasp of the victim's breathing permeated the tense air of expectation.

Then, slowly at first, but quickly gathering speed, the steady beat of tin plates punctuated the leaden atmosphere as the convicts hammered against their cell bars. A rhythmic cadence punctuated by dull grunts pulsated throughout the prison. Its intention was to send a message of hatred and disdain for the authorities of law enforcement.

Guards shuffled uncomfortably, rifles poised at the ready. They knew that a difficult night would follow. Reece Willard was a popular con. His obdurate refusal to be crushed beneath the boot heels of officialdom had struck a deep chord with the inmates.

The governor allowed the flagrant

demonstration of disapproval to continue for another minute. Then slowly he rose to his feet stubbing a cigar out under his boot heel. An arrogant smirk revealed teeth yellowed from too much baccy chewing as he cast a sneering glance across the courtyard.

'If this caterwauling does not cease immediately,' the raucous voice boomed out as Glasgow stroked the waxed tips of his moustache, 'my men will take five of you scum at random and give them each the same treatment meted out to the Mule.' He paused for effect. 'Except in their case, the punishment will be doubled.'

Again, the black gaze panned across the bleak expanse where Willard's lacerated body still hung. An atmosphere of defiance fanned back. Although it was significant that the rowdy display of disapproval had stopped just as suddenly as it had begun.

Much as the convicts sympathized with the Mule's plight, nobody had any desire to join him. And they all knew that Glasgow would not hesitate to carry out his odious threat. Such was his all-encompassing power. Hands resting on his ample hips, Governor Glasgow issued a nod of satisfaction before swinging on his heels and disappearing back to his office.

It was left for Warder Crow to cut the prisoner down and have him carried over to the grubby room that passed for a sick bay.

★ ★ ★

Willard slept well that night. That was primarily due to the care given to his brutalized frame by his Indian nurse. Wind That Talks was a member of the Northern Cheyenne. And it was she who had prepared a strong draught that knocked him out before she applied a cooling salve to his torn back.

More important, however, was the fact that she was the wife of warder Obediah Crow. Somehow, and to

Willard's good fortune, the governor had overlooked this crucial point.

The squaw's medical cupboard was full of herbs and potions that generations of Cheyenne medicine-men had proven to be effective remedies for all manner of ailments. Wind had further enhanced her craft in work she carried out under the auspices of the white eyes doctor at Fort Keogh. By combining the best of both worlds, she was able to handle most of the physical maladies that affected the prison population.

In particular, she had managed to prevent the spread of epidemics such as cholera and typhoid which could rapidly escalate in the closed environment of a prison.

Even Governor Glasgow was suspected of clandestinely seeking her aid for the containment of a decidedly personal infection contracted at Madam Syn's Whore House in the nearby town of Butte. One guard had made light of this to his colleagues. When Glasgow heard about this, the foolish guard suddenly disappeared. No further jests were thereafter openly exchanged.

So when prisoner 6715 was summoned the next morning, it came as a shock to witness the convict's miraculous recovery from the severe chastizement. Glasgow failed miserably to conceal his astonishment at the transformation when Willard was marched into his office.

For upwards of a minute he was stunned into silence. Willard gloated over the governor's discomfiture. Somehow he managed to contain the elation from showing on the grizzled features.

'Prisoner will stand to attention!'

The blunt command from his accompanying warder brought the nonplussed governor back down to earth.

Slowly, he rose from his padded chair. Gathering up a swagger stick, he strutted around the rigidly still form.

'It would appear that you have recovered quickly from your er . . . shall we say physical exercise yesterday,'

Glasgow sneered, poking Willard's back with the stick. The prisoner winced, drawing away from the jabbing.

'Stand still!' roared the guard.

'Perhaps Crow did not perform his duty as directed after all.' Glasgow completed the circuit. Arriving in front of the prisoner, he pushed his quivering snout up close to Willard's newly shaved visage. 'Maybe I should have the punishment repeated.' Then he sniffed the air. 'It appears that you have been well looked after since we last met.'

That was when the penny dropped.

'Ah, so,' he purred like a hungry mountain lion. 'Now I begin to understand. The squaw. She and I will need to have words. And perhaps a bit more besides.' A throaty chuckle erupted from the gaping maw. 'Yes indeed, she is a comely wench, even for a squaw woman.'

The governor tapped his leg with the stick considering the matter. Glasgow's leering threat was too much for the prisoner.

'Why you . . .'

A hand lifted to stop the flow of invective forced from between the prisoner's quivering lips.

'Don't even think of chastizing me, you heap of pig dung. One word and I'll have you tossed back into the Hole for the next six months.' Again the pudgy nose poked at the prisoner. 'And Crow will be out of a job.'

But then he remembered.

It was Crow's wife who had treated his whorehouse infection. And she had thus far remained silent on the issue. Get rid of her husband and the whole shameful episode would be out in the open. No. Wallace Glasgow would need to tread carefully.

The governor returned to his seat. His manner became more businesslike.

Opening a drawer, he removed a sack containing the prisoner's possessions that had been stored during his incarceration. From another he produced a gunbelt complete with the Remington Army revolver chambered for cartridge fire. He pushed the goods across the desk together with ten silver dollars.

'Upon release, all prisoners have their miserable goods returned, plus the princely sum of ten bucks to get you started back into civilian life.' Glasgow sneered, addressing the man standing before him. 'And don't go spending it all in the same saloon.' He chuckled at the witticism.

Willard deftly slung the shellbelt around his waist and fastened it. He palmed the revolver, giving it a nod of approval. Considering his lack of practice, the draw was adequate if rather stilted. Not surprising due to his lack of practice in recent years.

The gun swung towards the lounging governor.

Glasgow emitted a harsh guffaw. 'You surely didn't think I would be so stupid as to give you a loaded pistol, did you?' Removing the six shells from his pocket, he dropped them one at a time on to the desk. 'You can pick these up at the gate.' Then he addressed the guard. 'Now get this low-life out of here!'

Prisoner 6715 was summarily dismissed as Glasgow turned his attention back to the pile of forms on his desk.

Each released prisoner entailed a mountain of paperwork to be completed. It would still be another hour before this particular ex-con was just a bad memory. And that couldn't come soon enough for Wallace Glasgow. Willard had been a thorn in his side for too damn long.

The office door opened as the Mule was marched out. At that point, Glasgow looked up. Gruffly he called a halt. Adopting a more serious tone, he declared, 'And don't think to go after the guy that put you in here. That would mean a certain trip back with no chance of any remission. Then we'd be exchanging the whipping frame for a gallows and plot on Butte Hill.'

A casually raised hand dismissed the small procession.

They marched in line down the corridor, an armed guard on either side with another behind. Even at this late stage of a convict's incarceration, the pretense of order and regimentation still prevailed. The slightest infringement of the harsh discipline could mean a further period within the grim walls of Butte Penitentiary.

Willard had known a con who had laughed just before stepping outside of the external gate. The ecstatic euphoria of freedom overrode the poor sap's innate caution. That misdemeanour had earned him another three months inside.

Prisoner 6715 adopted his reputation as a stubborn mule. He fully intended that no such mishap would fall upon his squared shoulders. Maintaining a rigid stance, head held high, he marched in step with the guards. His arms swung in a steady rhythm, forcing the guards to do likewise so as not to lose face.

The governor's warning to curb his lust for vengeance resounded in his head as he drew ever closer to the final release. But it had fallen on deaf ears. In truth it had never left him since first arriving at Butte back in '68. Each and every day of his imprisonment had strengthened his determination to avenge the black-hearted deed that had put him in there.

Now that he was almost free, that resolution rang out in his head like a bugle charge.

2

Skulduggery

A snap of the whip and the prison wagon trundled down the hill towards the town of Butte.

The sharp crack made Willard recoil, the memory of his recent beating starkly resurrected. The searing pain on his scarred back had been eased by the Cheyenne nurse's ministrations. Only a dull ache now reminded him of the brutal punishment, and that would soon fade. Unlike the lattice of scars which would remain for a lifetime along with the burning desire for retribution that festered in his soul.

One other convict had been released along with Willard.

Known simply as Jackdaw, the old guy had a propensity towards acquiring all manner of junk and selling it on.

Not for cash which was of no value inside the prison. Services and favours along with extra grub and snout were the chief forms of currency.

That was how he had survived. When a convict needed something, be it new boots, soap or even pain killers, he sought out Jackdaw. The old jigger rarely failed to supply. He could even furnish the means to produce moonshine. Many were the times when cons needed to blank out their sorry lot by getting quietly inebriated.

The grey beard and thin straggly hair concealed a devious brain. Always on the scrounge, Jackdaw had been in the pen longer than any other convict. When anyone enquired what offence he had committed, he always tapped his nose secretly. By never revealing anything, it was inevitable that various rumours sprang up.

Some claimed that he had robbed a bank and hid the stash before the authorities could retrieve it. And until he revealed the location, his sentence kept being extended. Others said he had caught his wife in bed with his best friend and stabbed them both.

The most bizarre theory was that he had murdered his entire family and cut up their corpses before eating the body parts to hide the evidence. None of these stories were denied by the old reprobate. He merely nodded, chuckling uproariously as he went about the business of satisfying his latest request.

The two ex-convicts sat opposite one other in the wagon bed, each clutching the bag containing their meagre effects. No words were spoken. Both men peered back at the grimly austere structure that had controlled their lives for so long. The grey stone walls blotted out the morning sun, adding to Butte Hill's aura of menace.

Even the town in the valley below seemed to be overawed by its domineering presence.

In silence the journey down hill continued, each man lost in thought.

Willard was just thankful to have

finally escaped its heinously choking atmosphere. Now he could set about finding the rat who had been responsible for putting him there. The notion that by fulfilling that pledge he might end up in the pen's notorious cemetery never entered his head.

For Jackdaw, however, there were mixed feelings.

He had spent so long inside the bleak walls that being released came as a stark jolt to his system. A grim reminder that he would now have to stand on his own two feet. Prison life was habitual and strictly regimented. A strangely comforting routine of predictability.

Freedom on the other hand demanded that you think for yourself.

As the wagon jogged on down the hill, Willard cast his eye towards the hill on the far side of the town. A host of tents and temporary structures had sprung up. They were separate from Butte itself which nestled in the valley below.

A former Union soldier named Mike

Hickey had discovered seams of gold and silver up there just months before. He had quickly staked his claim at the assay office in Butte. Such events never stayed secret for long. And like many others before him, Hickey couldn't resist bragging about his discovery.

As a result, other prospectors flocked into the valley eager to seek their fortunes at the new strike. The news had even filtered into the prison system, passed on by the guards.

The mining camp was given the name of Anaconda.

But there was a far more lucrative metal beneath the surface, one that the mesmeric lure of gold and silver had overshadowed.

It was not until 1881 that the true value of the copper hill would be fully appreciated. A conglomerate headed by an astute businessman called Marcus Daly bought out Hickey's claim for a pittance. And by the end of the century the Anaconda was to become the world's largest producer of copper ore.

All this floated over Willard's head.

All he could think of as the wagon jogged onward was the circumstances that had led to his current situation. For seven long years, he had tried to work out the reason behind his so-called best friend's odious betrayal. What could have made Sam Foley shoot him down and leave him for dead?

Once again the details of the sordid episode that had landed him in the pen surged to the forefront of his thoughts.

⋆   ⋆   ⋆

It was a Wednesday afternoon on a hot July day back in the year 1868.

Dandy Sam Foley was sitting at his desk in the office above the Rolling Dice Saloon in Three Forks. The town lay fifty miles to the east of Butte. The trio of giant numbered cubes above the front entrance to the saloon were an obvious lure to frontiersmen ready and willing to gamble away their hard-earned paydirt.

The town lay on the Bozeman Trail that had been blazed in 1862 to aid the growing numbers of settlers heading west. It offered them protection from marauding bands of Sioux under the leadership of the wily Chief Red Cloud. To protect its citizens the government had built numerous military outposts along the trail which encouraged the rapid deployment of soldiers. One of these was close to Three Forks.

The town had originally grown up at a junction and bridging point of Sixteen Mile Creek. It lay in a broad fertile amphitheatre surrounded on all sides by towering ranges of Montana mountains. Snow dusting the highest peaks all year round looked like icing on a cake in the summer sunshine. Rich pastures of grass flourishing in the valley encouraged the growth of prosperous cattle ranches.

The prospectors were more recent incomers.

But they were all threatened by

Indians who resented this intrusion on to their tribal lands. Hence the importance of a strong military presence.

A grim expression clouded Foley's russet features. Well dressed in a midnight-blue suit and crisp white shirt, he enjoyed nothing better than strutting his stuff in the saloon bar to impress the customers. Not to mention the array of girls he employed to cater for more earthy needs.

Foley threw down the letter he had been avidly studying. Splashing a large measure of whiskey into a glass, he sunk the hard liquor in a single gulp. The firey spirit did nothing to calm the raging anger that was eating at his craw. In a fit of rage, he hurled the glass at the wall where it shattered into a myriad of fragments.

Seconds later the door flew open.

Sam's partner hurried into the room attracted by the clatter. Reece Willard had been checking the delivery of a new chandelier specially imported from Chicago. His face indicated his displeasure at learning the cost of what he considered was an unwarranted extravagance.

'What in tarnation is going on in here?' he demanded, clutching the invoice.

In contrast to his partner Reece always dressed down. He was quite content to wear range duds which he found more comfortable than the stuffy attire favoured by his dandified associate.

Foley was continually berating him for his lax sense of decorum.

'Dress like a hog and the punters will treat you like one,' Dandy Sam was frequently known to huff. 'Guys like us ought to set an example.'

Willard stared at the wet stain on the wall. Then at his partner. 'Some'n bugging you, Sam?' he pressed.

Foley pushed the letter across his desk.

'Read this!' he snapped. 'That slimy toad of a bank manager has only gone and foreclosed on our loan.'

Reece grabbed up the letter and quickly scanned the damning contents. 'He can't do that,' he railed wildly. The intended berating of his partner regarding the chandelier was forgotten. 'The contract we both signed gave us six months to pay that loan back. What's that conniving skunk playing at?'

He stalked over to the safe and opened the heavy door. 'We need to read that contract again.'

Delving inside, he pulled out a sealed envelope. Inside was an official document tied with pink ribbon. After perusing the details, his jaw dropped. 'What does it say?' enquired a worried Sam Foley.

For a full minute Reece was lost for words. He stared down at the spidery handwriting, all properly signed and sealed with the bank's red wax stamp. The partners' signatures were clear for all to see alongside that of Abner Montague, the bank manager.

Finally Reece stuttered out, 'Th-that wasn't the darn contract we signed up to. I'd never have put my name to those terms and conditions.'

After Foley had also read the contract, he shook his head in bewilderment. 'How did this happen? We both read it before signing.' A finger jabbed at the piece of dry parchment. 'And it says here that if'n we want more time, the rent will double for each extra month of credit allowed.'

'Ain't no way we can afford that, not after borrowing that money to expand the business,' concurred Reece. Removing his battered old Stetson, he dragged a limp arm across his sweating forehead. His face clouded over. A twisted snarl marred the handsome features as he spat back, 'We've been tricked. Montague has played us for a pair of greenhorn suckers.'

'But how did he do it?' protested Foley as he grabbed hold of the whiskey bottle and imbibed a hefty swig. 'You and me both read it through in full before signing. And this sure wasn't what we put our names to.'

Reece pounded a bunched fist into the palm of his hand. 'He must have had another contract drawn up . . . ' He paused, a glint of understanding registering in the caustic gaze. 'Yep, that's it. I recall now that he wanted us to sign three copies.'

'So how did he make the switch?'

'Don't you see?' urged Reece, pressing home the point. 'The genuine contract was on top with the other two hidden underneath with only the lower section on view. He must have kept the true copy at the bank along with the other fake.'

Foley interjected to complete the denouement. 'And we were given the false one all sealed up in an envelope. The shyster took it for granted that we wouldn't bother to read it again. After all, why should we?'

'The scheming rat!' Reece exclaimed, slamming an irate fist into the palm of his hand. 'Hand me that bottle!'

Reece Willard was not a hard-drinking man. But on this occasion he felt the need. The contents disappeared in a couple of gulps. As the hard liquor bit deep, his cheeks flushed.

'And I'd bet a royal flush to a pair of deuces that he burnt the real contract the minute we left his office,' growled his partner, helping himself to another slug. 'But what I can't figure out,' Foley mused, scratching his pomaded scalp, 'is why he would pull a stunt like this.'

'The price of land has risen sharply in the last year since the army arrived and that new gold strike was discovered up around Beaver Lodge,' suggested Reece. 'He could make himself a tidy sum with no outlay by forcing us out. I'm betting that the bank knows nothing about this bit of skulduggery. All the critter has to do is deny everything. What proof have we now to challenge his claim? As far as they're concerned, this piece of paper is a real contract.'

He threw the offending article down in disgust.

'So what are we going to do about it?'

enquired a dejected Sam Foley.

The unfamilar effect of the whiskey made Reece belligerent. He turned on his partner with a blunt accusation. 'Didn't I say we ought to tread carefully when dealing with the bank? Taking out such a big loan was your idea. Now look where it's gotten us. A half-finished dance hall and no way to pay for it.'

'Didn't hear any complaints when you put your moniker on that damn contract,' countered Foley, getting equally riled up. 'Reckon yourself to be such a smart cookie. So why didn't you spot the switch, eh?'

Reece had no answer to that.

He quickly simmered down, knowing that throwing out accusations left, right and centre was going to get them nowhere. A placatory hand was raised to ease down the growing tension between the two buddies.

'OK, OK,' he said. 'We've both been tricked. So there's no sense blaming each other. The question now is, how do we dig ourselves out of this god-damned fix?'

Further contemplation about the dire situation was shelved when a brisk knock came on the door.

3

A Plan Is Hatched

Without waiting for an answer, the door opened and a woman stepped into the room. Although sashaying would be a far more apt description of how Frenchie La Belle presented herself.

That was clearly not her real name. But nobody had bothered to make further enquiries when she had bounced on to the Three Forks scene some five months earlier accompanied by her entourage. Two wagons containing six dancing girls and all their costumes had come north from over the border in Wyoming. Frenchie had been forced out of Cody by a pompous town council that reckoned her show was too risqué for the sober citizenry.

This was the first town of any size encountered. With an army fort close by and new gold discoveries bringing in the prospectors, its potential for lucrative profits had been immediately apparent to the astute businesswoman.

Frenchie was as shrewd at negotiating work rates as she was at enthralling an audience. Flowing locks of fiery red hair matched a subtle wit that could easily squash the host of lurid comments flung out by drunken revellers. The two partners of the Rolling Dice Saloon had been equally smitten. As a result, Frenchie and her troupe had quickly been taken on.

Indeed, it had been she who had first suggested that the partners expand their enterprise by purchasing the empty premises adjoining the saloon and transforming it into a theatre and dance hall.

Sam Foley especially had been drawn to the exotic dancer like a moth to a flame. Transfixed by the smouldering eyes that hinted of paradise unbounded, fleshy lips that pouted evocatively and a full figure that oozed sex appeal, was it any wonder that she easily persuaded him to take the plunge?

Anything that could make a good profit was also supported by Reece Willard.

Neither of the two men, however, were prepared to admit that any woman, particularly a dancer, had swayed their decision.

None of that registered when Frenchie's alluring gaze rested on them. The morose atmosphere of moments before was quickly shrugged aside. Smiles of welcome concealed their burning anger.

'The bar could do with a large naked woman lounging on a sofa,' she announced breezily. Flicking a stray lock of hair off her alabaster features, she nonchalantly drew on a cigar encased in a silver holder.

Reece and his partner responded with stunned expressions. Their jaws dropped open. Frenchie chuckled gleefully.

'Above the bar, dummies.' Another bout of hilarity shook the dancer's ample bosom. 'What I meant to say was that you should think about employing an artist to paint one above the bar.' The two partners relaxed with a nod of understanding.

'You had us going there, doll,' Sam chided, with an admonishing wag of his finger and a wink towards his partner.

Frenchie continued with her attempt at persuading them to part with yet more money. 'They're called murals and are all the rage back east according to the fiddle player I just hired. Puts the customers in a good mood making them drink more and stick around longer.' She gave her effusive notion a nod of approval. 'Sound investment I'd say.'

She fastened her gaze on to Sam who had definately shown more inclination to heed her previous suggestions for increasing revenue.

Clearly in mind was the fact that

Sam Foley harboured romantic over-tures, more so than his partner. Bouquets of flowers, champagne sup-pers with violin accompaniment and imported chocolates spoke for them-selves. Indeed, Sam Foley was even contemplating marriage to the exotic temptress.

'So what do you think, boys?'

Much as he would love to have agreed to her suggestion, the practical reality of their dire financial circum-stances hung like the Sword of Damocles above Sam Foley's head.

Had she breezed in two hours before, Sam would have been putty in her hands. The artist would have been commissioned, and glasses of finest Napoleon brandy consumed to mark the occasion.

But things had changed.

Sam's mouth flapped. Desperately he tried to figure some way to wriggle out of agreeing to her proposal without causing offence. The last thing he wanted, even now, was to upset the woman he saw as his future bride. Neither did he want to reveal the shameful predicament in which he was now embroiled.

It was accordingly left for Reece to burst the bubble and take the blame for squashing Frenchie's exuberant scheme.

'It's a great idea, Frenchie.'

Reece paused. His drawled response was delivered with rather less enthusiasm than she had expected. At the same time, Sam Foley moved away supposedly checking on some paperwork to conceal his guilt-ridden features.

'Fact is though, at the moment we are experiencing what you might call a cashflow problem.'

'What's that supposed to mean?'

As expected, the dancer's reaction was decidely cool.

Reece hurried on, trying to appease the disappointed look on the woman's glossy façade. 'The new theatre has taken all our spare dough. Perhaps in a couple of months when it's up and running, we can reconsider.' He looked at Sam for support. 'Indeed, I am sure that Sam will want nothing more than a painted effigy of your good self over the bar when the time is right.'

'What the hell you talking about?' shot back the irate woman. Her feathers were well and truly ruffled at the intimation that she would want her naked contours besported for all and sundry to drool over. 'Is that what you think I am? A soiled dove with no self-respect?'

Tears spilling down her cheeks smudged the delicately applied make-up. Then she burst into tears. Sam arrowed a look of daggers drawn at his partner as he hurried across to try and calm the troubled waters. But the distraught woman was having none of it.

'Leave me alone,' she wept, shrugging off his clumsy attempts at mollification. Without another word, she hustled out of the room.

'Now look what you've gone and

done,' Sam complained bitterly. His fist opened and closed, muscles tight with vexation. 'Only gone and scotched it with the one dame I've ever felt like settling down with. If'n she drops me, I'll never damn well forgive you for this, Reece.'

'I didn't know you were that smitten with her,' protested Reece impotently, realizing that he was in the wrong. A pacifying attempt to calm the stormy waters followed. 'Don't worry, I'll make sure she knows that it was me and my big mouth that got things wrong. And that you had nothing to do with it. You'll see. By the end of the week she'll have forgotten all about it.'

'Let's hope so, buddy,' Sam grouched. 'Otherwise you and me are finished.'

'If'n we don't sort out this business with the bank we're finished anyway. I figure that's more important at the moment than your darned love life.'

Sam Foley could offer no repudiation to that slice of unwelcome truth.

He nodded in agreement, hooking

out a fresh bottle of whiskey from the cabinet behind his desk.

'So we're gonna have to work out some way to thwart Abner Montague's lily-livered chicanery.' Two glasses were filled to the brim. 'Got any suggestions, partner?'

With their friendship saved from an ignominious collapse, both men busied their minds to the task of solving the problem instigated by the felonious banker.

*　　*　　*

An hour later and the duo were still sitting across from one another. No words had been spoken as they nursed the bottle of whiskey. Grim lines of serious thought furrowed their brows as they struggled to figure out the next step forward.

Foley slammed a fist down on his desk in frustration.

'There's only one thing we can do,' he spat out. Reece waited for his partner to expand on the terse comment. 'Break into the bank and steal that bogus contract. Without that, there's no proof against us.'

Reece shook his head. 'What you're forgetting, old buddy, is that Montague will have registered it with the Montana Land Commission in Great Falls. No way will he have kept something like that here in Three Forks.'

Foley snarled, his frustration bubbling over. 'So what in thunder are we gonna do?' He stood and stamped around the room. 'No way am I about to let that thieving skunk steal what I've built up.'

'Don't forget that we're in this together,' Reece posited the cogent reminder.

'Sure, sure,' said Foley curtly. 'You know what I mean.'

'There is one way that we can get our own back,' Reece suggested tentatively. He paused, his gaze fixed on to an indeterminate point on the far wall of the room. Sam's proposal that they break into the bank had given him the idea.

'Go on, let's hear it,' hectored Sam, impatiently skewering him with a gimlet eye. He was ready to heed any practical solution to their dilemma.

'But it will mean giving up our holdings in Three Forks and heading for pastures new,' Reece continued. 'Are you prepared to do that?'

'Maybe,' Foley replied gingerly. 'Depends what you have in mind.'

'Well,' Reece sucked in a deep breath before launching into his plan. 'The bank lies just across the alley on our left, don't it?' Sam responded with a puzzled nod as his partner hurried on. 'It wouldn't take but a couple of nights' hard graft to dig a tunnel underneath. Then we could rob the safe and escape with a sizeable grubstake to get us started up someplace else far away from here.'

Reece hurried on, observing that the notion had begun to animate his partner. Sam's eyes were blazing. The thought of scotching Abner Montague's spurious scheme with one of their own made him laugh out loud.

'Now wouldn't that be something,' he chortled uproariously. 'His goose would be well and truly cooked. And it would serve the cheating swindler right. And I've always had a hankering to visit California.'

'It's Wednesday now. If'n we start on Friday, that will give us the whole weekend to break in, grab the dough and hightail it out of here.' Reece tempered his next comment with caution. 'It'll mean leaving everything apart from what we can carry.'

Sam's shoulders lifted in a shrug of resignation, accepting that this was their only way forward.

'Bow down to that bastard now, and we lose everything anyhow. He's left us with no other choice.' Then Sam posed a problem that neither had considered in their euphoria. 'How we gonna break into a heavy iron safe without using dynamite to blast it open?'

Reece gave the query a wry smirk. Tapping his nose he offered the perfect solution. 'What you don't know about me, Sam, is that I used to be a salesman for bank security products. And that included setting up safes. I reckon there ain't no locks or combinations that I couldn't master.'

'Well don't that beat all,' blurted out his surprised partner. 'Why didn't you tell me this before?'

'You never asked and there didn't seem any need . . . until now.'

Sam busied himself figuring out the logistics of the proposed enterprise. They couldn't just start digging on Friday night and hope to keep it a secret. It would require careful handling to prevent their employees getting suspicious.

'Frenchie mustn't get to know until we've got our hands on the dough,' Sam declared. 'Then I'll tell her. I know what you said, but I just can't leave her behind.'

'Hold on there, pard,' objected

46

Reece, raising a hand to curb Foley's unwelcome expectations. 'Only the two of us can be in on this caper. You want to haul a dame along, then count me out. The last thing we need is a woman slowing us down. Once Montague discovers the robbery and our sudden departure, all hell's gonna break loose. By then we need to be long gone.'

Foley bristled and fumed. He tried cajoling and wheedling to achieve his ends, finally resorting to threats. Jumping to his feet, he was all set for a fight. But Reece was quick to react. He pushed Foley back into his chair gripping both of his partner's wrists firmly.

Their eyes met. One set blazing with anger, the other focused and determined that sound reason should prevail.

'Simmer down,' Willard urged, standing over his choleric partner. 'Just think with your head and not your durned heart for once.'

Foley struggled to free himself, but

Reece was stronger. Keeping his voice calm and unruffled, he pressed his case for an objective and sensible resolution.

'You still want to make a go of it with Frenchie when we're in the clear in California, then send word for her to join you. Maybe she will, maybe not. But until then, we go it alone.'

Reece was adamant. A rigid stance and unblinking gaze assured the dandified saloon owner that his partner was not going to shift his view.

And with that, Sam Foley had to be satisfied. His twitching features relaxed as the ascerbic temper cooled down.

'OK, you win,' he muttered somewhat dolefully allowing Reece to loosen his iron grip. 'We'll play it your way.'

A restrained nod sealed the agreement although Foley was none too pleased. Indeed, he was harbouring suspicions regarding his partner's vehement assertion that Frenchie La Belle should not be a party to their scheme.

What was he up to?

Considerations on that score would have to be shelved. More important now was ensuring the successful completion of the robbery.

4

Betrayal

The next couple of days were tense. Frenchie could sense the fractious atmosphere. She tried raising it with Foley but he shrugged off her concerns blaming it on a difference of opinion regarding plans for the theatre.

In the meantime, the two partners had managed to bury their differences. They had sealed off the cellar. The reason given was rotting timber supports that needed replacing.

'I'll have the carpenter check it out on Monday,' Dandy Sam assured his bartender. 'You'll have to make do with bottles stored in vats of water if'n it's the cold stuff they want. Give everybody a discount to show our goodwill. That should ensure they don't seek their pleasures elsewhere.'

And Charlie Vickers had to be satisfied with that surety.

The jovial bartender often visited the cellar to change the beer barrels. The popularity of the Rolling Dice amongst the regular drinkers in Three Forks was its cold beverages. No other saloon in the town boasted a cellar. And in summer, a cold beer was like nectar from the gods to thirsty prospectors and army troopers.

Vickers didn't reveal that some pilfered bottles of finest Scotch were also stashed down there for his own private consumption. All he could do was pray that they were not uncovered. The bartender need not have fretted. The saloon owners had far more important issues to consider.

Ensuring there were no witnesses to their skulduggery, the partners surreptitiouly moved digging equipment down into the cellar.

It was a lucky break that the underlying ground was clay-based rather than the solid rock upon which most of the town was built. That feature of the landscape had enabled the cellar to be easily excavated when the saloon was constructed three years earlier. As such, the twenty-foot tunnel ought to present no problems.

Reece Willard in particular was loath to abandon their hard-won endeavour to the banking shark next door. He had invested the most money into the business. Leaving employees who had been with them from the start without a job was of little concern. They would easily secure other employment in the booming township of Three Forks.

Abandoning all that they had built up was a hard pill to swallow, but what other choice was there?

With no hope of repaying the loan in the time allocated on the false contract, they would lose the Rolling Dice and theatre annexe anyway. Better to grab some compensation before disappearing into the wide blue yonder.

For the umpteenth time since the shady solution to their quandary had been muted, he emitted a heavy sigh.

'Ain't having second thoughts are you, buddy?' enquired Foley, eyeing his partner's morose features from below beetled brows. 'That skunk Montague has given us no choice in the matter. This is the only way to make him pay for cheating on us.'

Reece's response was a disconsolate shrug of resignation.

'Don't mean I have to be happy about it,' he muttered, helping to move some barrels away from the side of the cellar wall nearest to the bank. A case of Scotch whiskey hidden behind was ignored.

Foley was more upbeat. 'Once we're on our way to California, ain't nothing to stop us setting up again with the grubstake Montague will have supplied.' He chuckled gleefully. All thoughts regarding their recent clash appeared to have been forgotten. 'I'd love to see that varmint's face when he discovers what's happened.'

'That sure would be a sight worth

seeing,' Reece agreed, chuckling.

At long last, Friday night arrived. The bank's doors had closed for the weekend and the two partners were itching to get started.

Yet they still had to maintain an outward display of bonhomie. Circulating throughout the saloon, they slapped backs and greeted regulars as if everything was normal. Just an ordinary Friday night like any other. An observant bystander might have wondered why they kept glancing nervously at each other and towards the large clock on the wall.

But nobody took any notice. Weekends were for whooping it up.

As the punters became ever more inebriated, Reece slipped away to begin his shift in the cellar. They had agreed to work in blocks of four hours. If any mention was made as to the other's absence, excuses could easily be formulated to allay any suspicion. And the noise of the house band and singing overhead would effectively stifle the noise made in the cellar.

Once the saloon closed its doors at one in the morning, both men went below and together put their backs into the hard graft. One slogged away at the tunnel face while the other shovelled the dirt back into the cellar. It was gruelling work in the dim light of the flickering lamps. But their combined efforts were rewarded.

By sun up, they had made excellent progress.

'Another night at this rate and we'll be right under the bank by Sunday morning,' Foley emoted with fervour. Glinting eyes pierced the dust-laden atmosphere. Sweat poured down his naked torso which heaved with the unaccustomed strain of the hard physical effort. Laboured breathing emerged in fits and starts. 'Ain't worked so hard in a coon's age. But it's gonna be worth it.' The thin lips drew back revealing a set of white teeth which beamed at his partner.

Reece couldn't help but become

drawn in by his partner's enthusiasm.

He smiled back. 'Time we were out of here before Charlie arrives,' he warned. 'See us like this and the guy will figure the place has been invaded by ghosts. Could give the poor sap a heart attack.'

Sam laughed, handing a cigar to his partner.

'And we could both sure do with a bath if'n I look anything like you.'

'Not to mention a well-earned double breakfast down at Ma Denton's Knife 'n Fork Diner,' Reece proposed, sucking on the thin tube of fine Havana tobacco. It tasted good. Perhaps their luck was going to change after all.

His whole persona rejected the need to leave Three Forks under a cloud. But he had convinced himself that this was the only way.

The next night continued the established pattern. Nobody suspected what was going on beneath their feet. Both men kept up the charade. Only once did the tricky problem of the vanishing partners raise its ugly head.

And it was Frenchie who brought up the subject.

'You boys never seem to have been around together this last couple of days,' she posited to Reece on the Saturday night when the saloon was in full swing. 'Something going on I should know about?'

Reece was taken aback by the sudden hint of suspicion. A brief shadow of alarm drifted across the handsome façade. But it was just as quickly diffused by a glowing smile of innocence.

His eyebrow lifted in feigned surprise. 'Can't say that I'd noticed. Sam's had business to conduct with Abner Montague about a loan that's in a delicate stage at the moment. We've both been over to his house to talk over the small print in the contract.' He shrugged knowing how close to the truth he was straying. 'That's all there is to it. Nothing to worry about.'

That appeared to satisfy the woman. Then she laid a hand on Reece's arm.

'You would tell me if anything was bothering you pair of horned galoots, wouldn't you?' The soft enquiry was a purring flow of concern as if Frenchie La Belle somehow knew that all was not as it seemed.

'Sure I would,' Reece assured her. 'Nothing to concern you in the least.'

He felt a deep sense of guilt uttering the blatant lie. Betraying her trust did not sit well. But their hands were tied. That skunk Montague had seen to that. For an instant he felt like blurting out the grim truth.

Thankfully, help was close at hand.

A sigh of relief issued silently through pursed lips as one of the dancing girls signalled across from the stage at the back of the room that the next performance was about to begin.

'Dolly wants you,' he said. 'Looks like you're on stage in five minutes.'

And with that the woman hurried off, much to Reece's relief.

* * *

It was around eight o'clock on the Sunday morning when Sam called back that he judged the tunnel to be directly under the bank manager's office.

'All we have to do now is dig upwards for three feet and bust through the floorboards,' he gushed excitedly. 'Then you can get to work on that safe.'

They had been working non-stop for four hours. Being Saturday night, the doors of the Rolling Dice had not closed until three in the early hours. There was no way of curtailing the usual hoohawing without causing a ruckus, not to mention reinforcing the suspicions of Frenchie La Belle.

Reece crawled down the constricted passage to join his partner. A candle flickered in the tomblike silence. All around, the cloying dampness pressed in like a suffocating blanket. There was barely room for the two men to move.

Sam stuck the spade in the roof of the tunnel. Immediately, a welter of damp clods poured down on to his exposed head. He coughed, hawking out a mouthful of dirt. A grubby hand wiped the clinging mire from his face.

'This is gonna be the worst part,' he spluttered. 'Good job there's only a few feet of it.' Another poke and more dirt tumbled down.

Reece used a rake to drag the fallen earth back down the tunnel into the cellar where the rest of the detritus was piled high. It took another hour to drive a square shaft upwards. Finally, the saloon owner's long-handled spade struck the wooden floorboards of the bank. A hollow echo incited a grim smile of satisfaction.

'We're there,' he called down the shaft. 'Bring up the ladder and hand me that drill to bore through the wood.'

By this time, Sam Foley was exhausted. He sank to the dank floor of the tunnel gasping for breath.

'You look plum tuckered out,' Reece observed. 'Rest up for a spell and have a cup of coffee while I take over,' he advised his partner.

Sam made no objections as he

crawled back down the tunnel.

Reece set up the small ladder and began work on the floorboards above.

A half hour of levering, drilling and riving followed before he was able to prise up the splintered boards. Without bothering to inform his partner, Reece crawled over the rim into the dark interior of an office. A sharp intake of breath followed. An anxious gaze scanned the room striving to pierce the stygian murk.

Slowly his eyes focused and he was able to make out the furniture of a room that he knew well. And for all the wrong reasons. They had indeed broken into the office of Abner Montague.

And there in the corner stood the all-important safe.

A dour look creased the dirt-smeared visage. He moved across to the iron casing to examine the locked door. 'No problem here,' he murmured to himself. 'This is where we turn the tables and get our own back,' Reece muttered under his breath. He slammed a bunched fist against the cold hard metal. 'You'll be laughing on the other side of your ugly mug come Monday morning.'

He scrambled back down the shaft to rejoin his partner.

'Broken through yet?' Foley asked, slurping a mug of hot coffee.

Reece helped himself to the large pot that had been simmering on the stove upstairs in the kitchen. He sunk a large draught before replying.

'We were spot on with the digging,' he said hurrying on to appraise Foley as to what he had discovered. 'And the safe should take no more than fifteen minutes to crack.' He put down the mug. 'I'll just go upstairs and get my bag of tricks.'

Foley gave the remark a puzzled frown.

'A security drummer never discards the tools of his trade.' With a wink and a nudge, he disappeared up the steps and out of the cellar.

Five minutes later he was back.

Both men crawled along the tunnel and up into the bank. An owl hooted in the distance, its muted call an ominous warning that time was passing. It might only be Sunday morning, the traditional day of rest, but they needed to be many miles south of Three Forks before the alarm was raised.

Without further ado, Reece hustled across to the safe. Extracting a set of strange implements he began probing the upper lock. Foley stood behind with an oil lamp raised overhead to give sufficient illumination for his partner to work his magic.

Steadily and with practised ease, Reece manipulated the skeleton keys until they were positioned correctly.

A wry smirk was thrown over his shoulder. 'Watch and gasp in awe, old buddy,' he chuckled, 'as you observe a maestro at work.'

Reece was actually enjoying himself. This was not the first time he had broken into a locked safe. In a past life, bankers and other businessmen who had mislaid their keys often needed his swift and expert assistance. Naturally a fresh lock had then to be fitted.

But this was the first time he had operated on the wrong side of the fence. And, surprisingly, it was turning out to be far more exhilarating than he had ever imagined.

Now he could fully understand why so many desperados thrived on their nefarious activities. It was not just the huge profits available. The thrill of bucking the system and escaping were equally potent incentives.

The lock clicked sharply in the quietude of early morning. Grasping hold of the handle, he paused briefly. A quick intake of breath, then he tugged downwards. The lock tumblers engaged and the heavy door swung silently open.

Both men automatically gasped.

Reece peered inside. His eyes lit up. There was far more dough inside than he had expected.

'Have we struck gold?' Foley asked, peering over Reece's shoulder. His voice was cracked and husky. A throaty cough punched out to hide his nervousness.

'Sure have.' Then Reece remembered. 'I clean forgot that it's month end. Payday for the army. That's why the safe is full to the brim with greenbacks.' Silence followed. 'You hear me, Sam?'

No answer. Reece made to turn round. And that was when stars erupted inside his head. A suffocating blackness enfolded him in its cloying embrace.

5

Welcome to Butte!

That was the last Reece Willard remembered until waking from a groggy sleep five days later in a prison cell. His body was swathed in bandages and he felt the hand of the grim reaper on his brow. The trial that followed once he had recovered was a foregone conclusion. Reece was found guilty and sentenced to seven years in the state penitentiary.

The trial was conducted *in absentia* as Reece was confined to the prison hospital. For the first two months of his sentence it was touch and go whether he would survive. But thanks to the ministrations of Wind That Talks, he had pulled through.

The small piece of lead that had done all the damage, however, was still lodged in his ribs. Removing it was considered too dangerous. Another quarter inch and the bullet would have ruptured his heart.

The uninvited guest gave him little trouble. Only the occasional twinge was a stark reminder of just how close he'd come to cashing in his chips. Each jolt to his system helped to focus his mind on the vengeance trail upon which he was now embarked.

A Wanted poster was issued for the apprehension of his partner who had escaped with the money. As far as he was aware from news passed down through the prison grapevine, Sam Foley had gotten clean away. Nothing had been heard about him since that catastrophic day.

So where was he going to start looking?

California was Sam's preferred choice. But that seemed too obvious.

So a return to Three Forks was the first step. Although what kind of reception he would receive was another matter. Reece stuck out his chin. He had served his time and could walk down the street with his head held high. The slate was clean as far as he was concerned.

The prison wagon rumbled to a halt outside a saloon. A huge pair of horns were affixed to the veranda. Above them, the name of Old Moses was emblazened in gaudy red and gold paint.

'End of the free ride, boys,' the guard called back over his shoulder. 'From here on you guys are on your ownsome. No more relying on us kind-hearted souls to service your every need. Now you gotta fend for yourselves.' He guffawed loudly at the joke.

Reece was still reliving his nightmare and how he had come to be incarcerated in Butte Hill.

The guard's gruff tones permeated his thoughts. He pointed to the large set of horns.

'That fella must have led upwards of fifteen herds up the Goodnight-Loving

Trail from Texas before he gave up the ghost.' A wistful expression cloaked the tough jigger's visage. 'I was ramrod on his last trek north from Austin. The old boy pegged out right here in the valley. A fitting tribute, don't you think, boys?'

Willard and his companion merely stared blankly at the object of the guard's gushing praise. They were more interested in getting into the saloon to slake a long-dormant thirst, the closeness of which was now making them salivate.

'You finished yammering on, Bridger?' rapped out Jackdaw. 'It's what's being served up in there that interests me and my pard far more than your darned memories.'

'No need to take that attitude,' grumbled the guard. 'Just saying is all.'

'If'n the job was so good, why'd you leave?' enquired the old guy stepping down off the back of the wagon.

'Looking after varmints like you pays a heap more,' Harvey Bridger scoffed, swinging the rig around and jouncing off back up the hill.

A suitable pair of obscene gestures followed his retreating back. Then the two ex-cons mounted the boardwalk. They were met by a large jasper brandishing a shotgun who barred their path. Marshal Tye Cushman was a grizzled lawman approaching fifty.

A careworn regard appraised the newcomers.

'You jiggers have until tomorrow morning to slake your throats,' he rasped. 'Then I want you out of here on the first stage. We don't cotton to ex-jailbirds hanging around our town.'

'We've paid our dues,' Willard snapped back acidly. 'And you got no right to order us around.'

Cushman took a pace forward. 'This gives me the right,' he growled, tapping the tin star pinned to his vest. 'And if'n you want to argue, then we can do it down at the hoosegow. I have a free cell just waiting for a mouthy bad boy like you.'

Reece had had enough of being

70

pushed around — seven years of it to be precise — and he was in no mood for jumped-up starpackers flexing their muscles around him. His fists bunched.

Jackdaw instantly read the signs. His hand reached out.

'Easy there, Mule,' he urged in a low voice. 'No sense in riling the marshal here. He's only doing his duty. Ain't that so, marshal?'

'You'd do well to heed your partner, mister,' smirked Cushman. 'Seems like he's got more sense than a jackass like you.'

Reece clenched his teeth, giving the overbearing lawdog the evil eye. But he remained silent, allowing himself to be led away.

Old Moses was a typical drinking den. Straw covered the wooden floor to absorb spilled beer. It looked as if it hadn't been changed for a week or more. Smoke hung in the fetid air, beams of sunlight arrowing through the thick atmosphere. And the smell. A blend of sweat and stale beer.

Jackdaw breathed in the heavy odour with relish.

'Don't that bring back heavenly memories, Mule?' he enquired of his associate as they sauntered over to the bar. 'Two cold beers and a bottle of whiskey,' the old guy ordered slapping one of his silver dollars down on the mahogany counter.

Guys with pasty faces were well known to locals in Butte. Prison incarceration was a dead giveaway. Three men at the far end of the bar nudged one another. Here was the chance for some fun.

Mudlark Brogan and his buddies were working a claim on the newly discovered gold field of Anaconda. They had just cashed in their latest stash of paydirt for US dollars.

Brogan sidled along the bar. 'We'd best keep our hands in our pockets, boys,' he called out loud enough for all patrons of the saloon to hear. 'Can't be taking any chances with common riff-raff around.'

'They don't smell too good either.' Arby Sinclair stuck his beaky snout in the air, sniffing imperiously.

'You sure are right there, Arby,' agreed Jonjo Billings. 'My old dog smells better'n that.'

Reece sighed. He should have known that this would happen so near to a prison. But after being warned off by officialdom, he had no intention of running from a bunch of tinpot miners. Slowly he swung to face the trio of burly roughnecks.

Carefully he hawked up the lump of tobacco he had been chewing and lobbed it at the boots of Mudlark Brogan. 'We might need a bath, mister. But you need some clean duds. This should help shine up your footwear. So I'd suggest that you get rubbing. Use that rag of a shirt on your back. Looks like that's all it's fit for.'

The smirk disappeared from Brogan's brutish features. It was replaced by an ugly snarl. Yellowed teeth were bared in fury. The irate prospector lurched forward reaching for the ex-convict.

But he had already imbibed a substantial quantity of liquor and his reactions were slow. Reece dragged the guy's hat down over his eyes. Drawing his pistol, he slammed the butt down on the exposed head. Brogan grunted and went down like a felled tree.

Witnessing their buddy's pistol-whipping, the other two surged forward.

Billings dragged a knife from a boot sheath. It glinted in the sunlight. A back-handed slash would have ripped open Reece's face had it connected.

The Mule saw it coming. He slewed back on his heels as the lethal blade whistled past his head. Catching the outstretched arm, he pulled the man off balance. His left shoulder slammed into Jonjo Billings' face breaking his nose. Blood poured from the injured proboscis.

Jonjo screamed. Backing off, he sank to his knees, both hands nursing the mashed injury.

Two men down, one to go.

The other patrons of the Old Moses had quickly dispersed. Eager to observe the fracas, they had no wish to participate. Especially when two of the antagonists had so quickly been eliminated from the fray. The barman had grabbed a shotgun from beneath the bar and was ready to use it should guns be brought into play.

Seeing his buddies getting the worst of the contest, Arby Sinclair had circled around behind Willard. Grabbing hold of a bottle, he stole up on the unsuspecting man who was bending down to retrieve the heavy knife. His arm lifted, ready to deliver a stunning blow to the back of the head.

Instead, he was pole-axed by another bottle. As soon as the fracas had started, Jackdaw had leapt over the bar. Now he joined in the affray with vigour. The bottle smashed over Sinclair's head, its liquid contents spraying the Mule's bent form.

Willard spun round as the thug

slumped to the floor at his feet. A finger reached up and tasted the dripping liquid.

'Waste of good whiskey, old-timer,' he remarked nonchalantly to his partner. 'But it was done in a good cause.' He offered a bow of acknowledgement to Jackdaw's timely intervention on his behalf.

'Figured these varmints were getting a bit too much for a young shaver like you,' countered Jackdaw, matching the other's wide grin. 'Thought it only right that I helped you out.'

The end of the uneven altercation elicited a babble of chatter as it was discussed. The bartender put away his gun, and the two ex-convicts toasted one another.

'Perhaps now we can enjoy our drink in peace,' sighed Reece, raising the beer mug to his lips. But he never got to sample the amber nectar.

The brusque but well-known bark of Marshal Tye Cushman cut through the sweaty atmosphere.

'I might have figured you jaspers couldn't keep out of trouble,' he snapped. The solid bulk of the lawman filled the doorway of the saloon. In one hand a cocked pistol, in the other the deadly scatter-gun. And both were pointed at the two ex-convicts. 'That will cost you both a fine of five dollars, or spend a month in the hoosegow. It's your choice.'

Dark eyes bored into the startled men.

'But it was these turkeys that started all the ruckus,' protested Reece. A sweeping arm indicated the groaning forms wallowing in the grubby straw. 'All we wanted was a quiet drink.'

'What do you have to say, Chance?' enquired the lawman of the bartender. The rotund 'keep shrugged. 'All I saw was these two setting about Mudlark and his buddies for no good reason.'

Reece swung an angry face towards the lying toad. 'Why, you no-good skunk . . . ' He reached across the bar to grab the simpering beer-puller.

But Jackdaw quickly placed a restraining arm across his chest. 'Leave it, Mule. These guys have got us in a headlock. A well-planned ambush if ever I saw one. They've clearly pulled this kind of stunt before. In fact, I'd say it was a regular thing to hustle ex-cons trying to start out afresh.' He pulled the other man towards the door. 'Don't worry, Marshal, we're going. Wouldn't want to stay in a dump where we ain't welcome.'

The lawman barred his path. Holstering his pistol, he held out a hand. 'Well? Is it gonna be the fine or the pokey?' The shotgun jabbed the old-timer's belly.

Jackdaw fished out the shiny new coins and counted out five which he handed to the crafty starpacker.

Reece held the lawman's arrogant gaze while he slowly did the same.

Then they pushed past the smirking varmint on to the dusty street.

Loud guffawing erupted inside the Old Moses as the patrons helped up their injured associates. Fresh drinks were pushed on to them.

Four men remained seated at the back of the room. They had been idly playing cards while the ruction was in progress.

The men were staying at the Prairie Palace Hotel across the street. They had been in Butte for the last week awaiting the next release of prisoners from the penitentiary.

'That's him,' Geyser Bo Joplin informed his three sidekicks. 'The tall lean critter in the black Stetson. The boss gave me a detailed description before we left Medicine Hat.'

A hard-nosed tough, Joplin hired out his muscle to the highest bidder. He had acquired his unusual sobriquet due to a quick temper. It had a tendency to flare up, just like the Old Faithful hot spring in Wyoming.

'Who's the old dude then?' asked a raw-boned tough, sporting a livid scar down the left side of his face. The old knife wound dragged his features down to one side giving him a permanent scowl. Boise McCabe lifted his skeletal frame out of the chair.

'Must be just another ex-con,' propounded the third member of the group. Beavertop Baker had been a trapper who had given up the tough life in the mountains for the more lucrative profession of a bounty hunter. However, he still favoured buckskin apparel and the fur hat that had given him his nickname.

The fourth member of the gang was a half-breed Sioux whose father had been an army scout. Known simply as Dakota, which was his tribal home, he maintained a dignified silence most of the time. He only deigned to speak in stilted English when the need arose. At other times he mumbled away in his own tongue, much to the exasperation of his associates.

'He seemed mighty handy for an oldster,' McCabe contributed with respect.

'Don't bother about him,' interjected

Joplin impatiently. 'It's Willard that concerns us. Let's go see what he's planning to do now. The boss said to follow him and if'n he heads east for Three Forks to let him know by telegraph. Then he'll give us fresh instructions.'

6

Foley Takes Action

For the last two months, Sam Foley had become morose and waspish. A bad temper and surly responses to all and sundry had become his normal behaviour. Employees tiptoed around him, wary of upsetting the petulant saloon owner. And nobody had plucked up the courage to question him about it.

Foley was alone in his office, nursing a bottle of whiskey.

He adjusted the new spectacles that had been prescribed by an oculist in Great Falls. Every time there was a rap on the door, the specs were removed. It wouldn't do for the hired help to know that Dandy Sam Foley's eyesight was failing. His line of business demanded a tough exterior. Any weakness would be exploited and used against him.

It had begun when Sam was delivering a land acquisition contract to a lawyer in Moose Jaw. His horse had stepped in a gopher hole and broken its leg. The injured nag was disposed of with a bullet in the head. But it left Sam cast afoot. As a result he had been forced to walk to the nearest trading post at Pinto Creek.

Three days without shelter in the scorching heat of the Great Sandy wilderness had taken a heavy toll.

The blistered face and a dehydrated body had recovered. But Sam's eyes had been permanently scarred.

Spectacles were deemed essential to conduct his everyday business interests. Only the previous month, another trip to Great Falls had been necessary to acquire a more powerful pair of lenses. The papers lying on his desk blurred. Sam was forced to squint in order to read the small print. He cursed under his breath.

But there was something else that was bugging him. Something far more serious. Something that could threaten his continued existence.

Sam Foley's ex-partner was due for release from the Montana State penitentiary within weeks.

And Foley was worried.

Ever since learning that the bullet despatched from his Derringer had not done its job of termination, he had cursed his ineptitude. Why hadn't he taken the time to check that Willard was a goner? The gun held two bullets and he had only used one. Time and again during the last seven years, he had damned his stupidity. He had blamed it on the tension of the moment, his need to grab the dough and get clean away.

Seven years in the pen had seemed like a long time then. But now it had come to an end, as he knew it always would.

The double-crosser had experienced no hitches on his flight north of the border. He had settled in Medicine Hat. The stolen money had financed a new enterprise. The heist had provided more than enough to buy a well-established business and expand, just like he had sought to do in Three Forks.

Foley splashed a generous measure of Scotch into a glass. His mind was in turmoil. What should he do about Reece Willard?

He had wracked his brains trying to think if there was anything that could lead the guy to the Canadian province of Alberta. No clues had been left, and nobody knew he was up here.

Perhaps he was worrying unduly. If Willard had any notion of revenge in his mind, logic said he would head south-west for California. That was where they had planned to start up again.

Heading north had been a stroke of genius.

Nevertheless, as long as the critter was breathing, Dandy Sam Foley could not rest easy.

Yet something deep inside his subconscious was urging caution. Or was it guilt? Perhaps seeing his own mortality threatened by the onset of blindness had made him assess what truly mattered in life. Indecision clouded his judgement. Knowing Reece Willard as he did, Foley was convinced his ex-partner would seek retribution. And who could blame him?

He sank the hard liquor in a single draught. It barely touched the sides of his throat. But what it did do was focus his mind on to the course of action that had to be taken to bring him peace of mind.

He pulled a bell rope beside his desk. It was an innovation he had had installed to summon anybody within the premises of the Dice Roll saloon and gambling palace.

A magazine left by a visiting party of hunters had extolled the virtues of such a system that was commonly in vogue in English stately homes. That had appealed to Sam's vanity. Having English blood in his veins, he naturally aspired to aristocratic pretensions.

A minute later there was a knock at the door.

Sam quickly removed his spectacles and stuck them out of sight in his pocket.

'Enter,' he announced, in an imperious voice.

A thin wisp of a man hustled into the room.

'You called, boss?' enquired the fawning tones of Jethro Punch.

The little guy was a weed to look at, but he possessed a sharp brain. With Punch in charge of his financial ledgers, Foley was confident that there would be no pilfering such as he knew had gone on at the Rolling Dice in Three Forks. And the guy was no milksop. When offered the job of book-keeper, Punch had demanded a hefty salary.

Foley was initially reluctant to comply. But the guy had more than made up for his high price tag. The saloon owner had no regrets.

'Is Geyser Bo around?' he asked.

'Him and Beavertop Baker have gone

up to Elkhorn collecting rents,' replied Punch without hesitation. He made it his business to know the whereabouts of all Dandy Sam's employees. 'They should be back this evening.'

'Send them up here pronto, as soon as they get back,' ordered Foley. 'And emphasize that it's urgent. I don't want those chuckleheads trying to drink the place dry. They have serious business to conduct.'

Punch did not question the directive. And Foley did not elucidate. But he knew it would be carried out. He nodded his approval, handing the little dude a cigar. A lordly flick of the head indicated that the meeting was over.

★ ★ ★

'Where you planning to go when you leave here, Mule?' enquired Jackdaw, tagging along behind his associate as he moseyed along the boardwalk of Butte's single main street.

'I'm headed for Three Forks. But first

stop is a decent meal at the diner I saw up the street as we drove in.' Reece shot his buddy a caustic frown. 'And quit calling me by that moniker. It was OK in the pen. But out here it's just plain old Reece Willard. Anything to remind me of that durned hell hole will be buried in the past where it belongs.'

The little weasel nodded. 'Sure thing . . . Reece. But I'm still Jackdaw. Always have been and always will be. I can't recall my birth name it's so danged long since I heard it.' He paused before adding, 'Mind if'n I join you? I could murder a prime rib-eye smothered in fried potatoes with green beans and sweet corn . . . '

'Hold it there, fella,' Reece admonished the old guy. 'You're making my mouth water and we don't know yet whether we can afford it.'

'I'll wash dishes if'n I have to. And you can dry.' Jackdaw's mouth split in a wide grin.

'Then what are we waiting for?'

Side by side, they breezed off to the

Coffee Cup Eating House. Both were slavering at the mouth just thinking of their first decent meal in a sackful of moons.

The four hardcases watched them go. Then they went back inside the Old Moses and took a table by the front window.

'We'll follow them soon as they've finished at the diner,' declared Geyser Bo eyeing the man beside him. 'I reckon it's your shout for the drinks, Beavertop. And make it a bottle of the good stuff.'

Baker grunted before hustling over to the bar.

It was an hour later before their two marks left the Coffee Cup. A dreamy expression softened Jackdaw's heavily furrowed visage. His younger associate shook his head in wonderous appreciation. They were both stuffed to the brim.

'That was the best steak I ever tasted,' murmured Reece, lapping his tongue across pursed lips.

'And that apple pie . . . ' gurgled his buddy.

' . . . just melted in the mouth,' Reece concluded. 'And now for a cigar to finish off.'

He handed Jackdaw a Cuban Original and lit them both as the two men sat down on chairs outside the diner. A waitress appeared with two china cups and saucers together with a pot of the establishment's own brand of coffee. She set it down on a low table.

'Enjoy the meal, sirs?' enquired the pert young girl.

Gentle sighs and smiling nods of esteem accompanied by a fifty-cent tip sent the girl off with a smile of her own.

For five minutes, the two unlikely diners just sat and wallowed in the luxury of repletion and the freedom to enjoy it. The splashout had, however, severely dented their resources. They were now left with only a silver dollar apiece. Hardly enough to finance bed and board in a flop house, let alone a protracted expedition in search of

Dandy Sam Foley.

A cloud drifted across the avenger's craggy façade. Most important was to solve the mystery as to why the bastard shot him in the back and left him for dead — a heinous betrayal for which there could be only one outcome. Reece's hand slipped down to the revolver on his hip.

But for a few minutes at least, all that was forgotten.

It was Jackdaw that finally brought the reality of their situation home to roost. 'You mentioned heading for Three Forks. Ain't the bank in that berg the one you robbed?'

A stony expression greeted the enquiry.

'Too many questions, old-timer,' Reece cautioned as he strode down the street to the Overland Stage office. 'You never heard the one about curiosity and the cat?'

'Curiosity is what first got me the name of Jackdaw. And I'm still here, large as life and twice as ugly.'

Reece couldn't help but laugh at the old guy's wit. But he still didn't clarify his reasons for travelling to Three Forks.

'Time I was booking that seat on the stage,' he said rising to his feet. 'Where are you making for then, Jackdaw?'

The old scrounger shrugged. 'Ain't much thought about it,' he mumbled, automatically following in his young associate's shadow.

When they reached the office, Jackdaw laid a restraining arm on Reece's shoulder.

'I ain't got no plans of my own,' he said in a temperate murmur. 'So . . . ' He paused before revealing what had been brewing in his crafty brain. 'Mind if'n I mosey along with you for a spell?'

Reece eyed the little guy with a quizzical regard. He hadn't given any serious thought to taking on a partner. Indeed, the task of hunting down his ex-friend and business confederate was one that he preferred to handle alone.

Jackdaw took advantage of the other

man's hesitant reaction.

'Didn't I just help you out in the saloon? And I could be your eyes and ears in Three Forks where folks will be watching your every move.' Taking a quick breath, he hurried on before any objections to his proposal could be vented. 'I know which way to point a gun as well as being handy with my fists, and other things.'

He was referring to the crack of the whiskey bottle over Arby Sinclair's head. 'And you're gonna need someone to nose out the lie of the land, so to speak, when you get there. Someone who ain't under suspicion.'

Reece was taken aback by his buddy's fervent supplication.

Maybe the old guy was right. Another person could help him out. Everybody in Butte Hill was aware of the bizarre circumstances that had led to Reece Willard's incarceration. And he had made no secret of his intention to seek revenge upon release.

'OK, you can ride along,' he agreed

after due consideration. 'But this ain't gonna be no Sunday school picnic. I'm out for vengeance and that means bullets are likely to fly. You ready to face a loaded gun?'

'I sure ain't no tenderfoot, boy,' Jackdaw remonstrated vehemently. 'Most of my life has been spent dodging from one tight corner to another. There's a canny brain up here.' He tapped his jutting head. 'And that's just as useful as a fast draw.'

'Guess you're right at that,' nodded Reece offering his hand. 'Shake on it then . . . partner.'

A grin wider than the Rio Grande cracked the old guy's lined features.

Together they pushed open the door of the Overland office and walked in. A bald-headed clerk with a pencil stuck behind his ear looked up from the ledger he was studying. Wally Flood was in a less than cheery frame of mind. His stable lad had gone off sick, and the stage had to be prepared for the next run the following day.

'Can I help you gents?' he asked in a surly tone of voice.

'When does the next stage to Three Forks leave?' Reece enquired.

'You're in luck, mister,' the clerk replied. 'The weekly mail delivery departs tomorrow morning at ten sharp, and I have two seats left.'

'We'll take them,' said Reece.

'That will be four dollars each.' The clerk held out his hand to receive payment before making out their tickets.

Reece looked at his partner. Jackdaw's mouth fell open. The clerk peered from one to the other over the spectacles perched on his beaky snout. He sensed a mood of reluctance.

'Eight dollars for the pair if'n you please.' His tone had hardened.

'That might be a problem,' muttered Reece haltingly, 'seeing as we only have two bucks between us.'

The clerk's nose twitched. Knowing that he would have to work half the night getting the stage ready had soured

96

Wally Flood's mood. And now these two down-at-heel layabouts were trying to hustle him.

'Eight dollars or walk,' he snapped.

A glint appeared in Jackdaw's frosty gaze.

'How about if'n we ride up top.' He hurried on before the clerk could utter a refusal. 'In addition, we'll muck out the stables tonight, and help your ostler get the stage ready in the morning.' A doleful gaze pleaded with the clerk to loosen his britches. 'Surely a neighbourly guy like yourself can see that has to be a fair deal for two travellers down on their luck?'

The clerk's imperious mood lightened. A heavy load had suddenly been lifted from his shoulders. Now it was Lady Luck sitting there. But he didn't let it show on his rotund features. Wally mulled over the old tramp's suggestion as if it was a difficult decision to make. Stroking his fleshy chin, his features contorted into various ornery grimaces.

Then slowly, the pretentious charade

was phased out.

'Could be we have a deal,' he said in a measured way. A jabbing finger pointed at Reece. 'Provided this young fella here rides shotgun. We've been having trouble with road agents on that run. And the company ain't seen fit to employ anybody as yet.'

'Sounds good to me, mister,' Reece concurred, without hesitation, as the two buddies handed over their money. No tickets were required and the money went straight into Wally Flood's pocket.

Now the two partners were stone broke with only the duds they stood up in. But at least they had a bed for the night, even if it was only in a livery stable. The next stage of the quest could be dealt with when they reached Three Forks.

They followed the directions given by Flood to find the stableyard which lay on the edge of the town. It had been erected just outside the town limits in order to avoid the company having to pay ground rent.

Bo Joplin's beady eye pursued the two men down the street as they headed for the Overland stable.

'You jaspers wait for me while I go make some enquiries as to where those critters are headed,' he told his sidekicks. 'Got me an itch in my foot that tells me this ain't gonna be what the boss wants to hear.'

He was back inside of ten minutes. A scowling twist did not denote good tidings. 'They're headed for Three Forks in the morning.'

'That ain't south-west for California, it's east,' remonstrated Beavertop.

'And it's sure not the direction that Foley was expecting him to take,' agreed Boise MacCabe. 'What we gonna do about it, Geyser?'

'The boss's instructions were clear,' Joplin declared firmly. 'If'n he makes for Three Forks, we were to deal with the varmint.'

Sam Foley had not in actual fact ordered a killing. His instructions were merely to follow Willard and report his movements. But Joplin had decided early on that such a course of action was a waste of his time. Get the job done quick, no frigging about, then back to Medicine Hat and a big fat bonus.

The hardcase had convinced himself that such a course of action was what the boss really wanted.

'You mean kill him?' asked McCabe.

'What do you think, dummy?' rapped Joplin. 'It don't mean we slap the jigger on the back and buy him a drink.'

'How you planning on handling it then?' cut in Baker. The others always looked to Geyser Bob for answers.

'Ain't got that sussed yet,' mused Joplin pensively. 'We'll go back to the Old Moses and work something out over another bottle of Scotch.'

7

Night Prowler

The two ex-convicts didn't finish their work until one in the morning. Mucking out the stalls, feeding the horses and loading up the Concord stagecoach for the next day's run found them both plum tuckered out.

Jackdaw threw himself down on a heap of straw.

'I ain't worked this danged hard since the spell I did on a chain gang before the War. That was down Texas way,' he gasped out, eyes closed and mouth open wide sucking in lungfuls of dung-scented air. His bleary eyes closed as much-needed sleep wrapped itself around his tired old frame.

Reece cast aside his pitchfork and joined him.

'What was that for?' he asked settling

down into the comforting warmth of the fresh straw.

'I was working as a faro dealer in San Angelo.' The old guy's rheumy eyes flickered open as he thought back. 'Had me something going with the leading dancer of a troupe called the Starlighters.' The recall seemed to jolt him back to life. 'Boy, she was one heck of a looker. Little slip of a gal by the name of Lilly May. You'd never guess to look at me now that I was a tough, good-looking fella in those days, would you?'

Reece smiled but made no comment. He waited for the old guy to continue. The dreamy reminiscence suddenly hardened.

'I caught the low-life skunk of a town mayor forcing himself on her one night after the saloon had closed. The rat had gone to her room and pushed his way in.'

'What did you do?' asked an enthralled Reece Willard who was now fully caught up in the quirky past antics of his partner.

Jackdaw shrugged. 'Roughed him up some, then threw the bastard out of the window.' He chuckled aloud at the recollection. 'He landed in a muck cart that was passing at that very moment.'

Another raucous guffaw.

'Phooogh!' Jackdaw held his nose. 'He didn't get rid of that stink for a week. Doing this job was what brought it to mind after all these years. Problem was that important guys like the mayor have influence. So it was him that was left smiling in the end when I got a spell on that chain gang.'

'That's one heck of a tale, Jackdaw.' Reece threw a rather sceptical look at his buddy. 'You sure that imagination of your'n ain't working overtime?'

The old-timer puffed up his shoulders, indignation at the slur clouding his lined face. 'You calling me a liar, son?' he bristled.

Reece held his hands up in surrender. 'If'n you say so, then I believe you. It just seems a might farfetched, is all.'

'Well it sure is the goddamned truth,'

stressed the fiery little weasel. 'And I'll wager they're still talking about it in San Angelo to this day.' Soon after that, they both fell asleep. Dead to the world.

* * *

The four shady characters led by Geyser Bo Joplin had not made any headway as to their next move when the saloon closed its doors for the night. The three white men headed back to the Prairie Palace to sleep on it. Being of Indian descent, custom forbade Dakota from being permitted to stay in a hotel.

He left the others and made his way back to the livery barn where he had been allowed a corner in the hayloft. It was as he was about to enter the barn that he heard voices. The half-breed paused on the threshold, listening intently. The men inside were those they had been sent to follow. And they were about to settle down for the night.

Here was a golden opportunity to

gain some much-needed prestige from the rest of the gang. Returning to the hotel, he persuaded the reception clerk to summon Geyser Bo to come down.

'What's bugging you now, Dakota?' grumbled Joplin as he trundled down the stairs, pushing his shirt back into hastily donned pants. 'Ain't you had enough firewater for one night?'

The Indian gestured for Joplin to follow him outside. What he had to impart was not for the wagging ears of a nosey receptionist. The gang leader followed with reluctance.

'Men we seek staying in barn.' The deeply sonorous pitch was like the tolling of a funeral bell. 'Another hour and they easy to kill.'

Joplin's eyes gleamed in the moonlight. 'Well done, kiddo,' he commended his associate. 'That would solve all our problems in one fell swoop.' The devious brain set to work, figuring out a plan of action. 'And this is how we'll do it,' he decided after a few minutes of fervid contemplation.

It was around three in the morning when Dakota and Beavertop Baker cautiously opened the barn door. They paused inside, listening intently. Nothing moved. The only sound to disturb the silence was the howling of a coyote in the distance. Inside the barn, the steady rumble of a low snore from the far side of the barn in one of the stalls indicated where their quarry was sleeping.

Baker smiled, pointing to where the noise had its origins. Inside the barn, the blackness was complete. They would have to proceed with stealth and care. No problem for Dakota who was well versed in such tactics. He moved to the left while Baker stepped right.

Slowly and with infinite caution they neared the sleeping forms. On the far side of the barn, streamers of moonlight beamed through narrow gaps in the slatted walls.

The two sleeping figures were bedded down in the end stall. One of them rolled over. Baker froze, holding his breath. A snort cut through the heavy silence. Then Jackdaw settled down into a new position. Baker's confidence increased as he drew closer. Carefully, he extracted a knife from the sheath strapped to his boot. It felt good in his hand. He grinned wolfishly.

Dakota was just behind him, his eyes focused on the unsuspecting body of the old reprobate. His own knife rose as he bent over the slumbering figure.

Then it happened. One of those unforeseen strokes of bad luck.

Baker failed to spot the pitchfork that Jackdaw had left leaning against the outside of the stall. His boot caught it. The implement clattered against a tin bucket. Baker stumbled. His hand reached out and grabbed some hanging bridles which rattled against the stall.

The game was up.

Reece instantly threw off the lethargy of sleep. Spotting the dark shape reeling over him, he grabbed the pistol that lay inches from his hand. Three shots were hauled off in rapid succession. Orange tongues of flame lit up the interior of the stable.

Baker clutched at the bleeding holes in his chest as he staggered back. He tripped over the fallen bucket and crumpled to the floor. In the meantime, realizing that their murderous plan had failed, Dakota slipped away, losing himself amidst the shadowy recesses. A door over to the left banged. Two more shots pursued the fleeing Indian.

But Dakota had made good his escape.

'What in thunder is going on?' yelled the distraught figure of Jackdaw. The gunfight was over before he knew what was happening.

'Seems like we had some unwelcome visitors.' Willard indicated the slumped outline of the dead man. 'His sidekick managed to escape.'

Scrambling to his feet, Willard dashed over to the creaking door and peered out into the stygian gloom. His gun panned the blurred vista. But there was nobody in sight. The noisy ruckus, however, had not gone unnoticed.

Minutes later, the burly figure of Marshal Cushman hustled round the corner of the barn. When he saw who was involved in the set-to, the lawman couldn't resist a corrosive barb. 'Can't keep out of trouble, can you, buddy?' The snide remark rankled Willard who fumed with anger.

'Me and my pard have just been ambushed in our sleep, and all you can do is try to put the blame on us. It was only luck that I woke up in time.' He paused to draw breath before continuing the fiery retort. 'What sort of a tin pot town is this to vote in a starpacker like you?'

Now it was Cushman's turn to display rancour. 'I ought to run you in for vagrancy,' he threatened brandishing the shotgun.

'But you won't, eh Marshal? 'Cause I'd be forced to reveal what really happened.' Willard's face cracked in a tight smile that lacked any humour, much to the discomfiture of the devious lawdog. 'Innocent travellers have been attacked. Why don't you do your job and find the culprit who escaped?'

Tye Cushman attempted to back-track knowing that he had overstepped the mark. Scratching a vesta on the wall, he ignited a lamp and peered down at the dead body. 'Never seen this guy before. What about you two?'

Both men shook their heads.

'Looks like an opportunist robber to me who saw you bed down in here and figured to try his luck,' the lawman intimated. 'I'll keep an eye open for his partner.'

'Perhaps at the same time you could arrange for the undertaker to remove this jasper,' suggested Reece.

Cushman reasserted his belligerent manner. 'Just make sure that you and your buddy are on that coach in the morning.'

'We will be, Marshal, have no fear on that score,' scoffed Willard at the disappearing back. 'Ain't no chance of us hanging around in this dump.'

Once the lawman had departed, Jackdaw posed the question that had also been bugging Reece. 'Who do you suppose really tried to kill us?' he queried as they ambled back to the stall and its new grisly occupant. 'That theory of Cushman's is all hogwash. What have we got that anybody would want to steal?'

'You're right, Jackdaw,' agreed Reece. 'Could be those dudes that caused us trouble in the saloon. But this fella wasn't one of those.' He raised his hands in bewilderment.

Five minutes after being swallowed up by the night, Dakota flitted up the back stairs of the hotel. Silently he pushed open the door at the end of the first floor corridor and entered a room on the left.

Joplin was pacing up and down, anxiously awaiting the return of his sidekicks. McCabe was lounging on the bed. Both men were nervously smoking cigarillos.

'Where's Beavertop?' spat Joplin, immediately sensing that all had not gone according to plan.

For once the Indian's blank mask of stoicism slipped. He blurted out the recent events in staccato bursts. Arms waving like windmills, he struggled to forcefully convey the idea that the misadventure was all Baker's fault.

Joplin was not ready to accept excuses. 'You durned fool!' the gang leader rapped, his face purple with rage. A savage backhander struck the Indian across the mouth. Blood dribbled from a cut lip. But Dakota just stood there, forced to accept the humiliating treatment. 'Did anybody spot you?' Joplin added.

Dakota shook his head vehemently. 'Disappear when Beaver get shot. Nobody see in dark.'

'At least, we won't be under suspicion,' said Joplin, calming down as he considered how best to proceed. He sucked hard on the stogie to concentrate his thoughts. 'Ain't nothing we can do until morning.' He peered at the half-breed, contempt oozing from every pore. 'You'd best take Beavertop's bed seeing as he ain't got no more use for it.'

Back in the stable, the two hands took some time to settle the frightened horses. The rest of the night was divided into watches. In the unlikely event that the surviving bushwacker returned to complete his unfinished business, the two ex-convicts did not intend being pinned down by the wrong end of a bowie knife again.

Sheer exhaustion, however, took its toll. By the early hours, both men had succumbed to the soporific attentions of Morpheus.

It was the dawning call from a neighbourly cockerel that woke them at first light. The dead body was still where it had fallen. The two men tried to ignore the rancid odour of death that hung in the air.

A splash of water from a fire bucket helped dust off the cobwebs as they went about the task of feeding and watering the team of six and settling them in the traces. The animals were still a mite skittish following the night's work of the Grim Reaper.

That job completed, it was over to the Coffee Cup for a full breakfast. Another perk that Jackdaw had wheedled out of the stageline agent. It had involved showing Flood how to obtain double the light from his tallow lamps by regularly cleaning and trimming the wicks.

During their meal, the solemn figure of the undertaker appeared from the direction of the stable. He was accompanied by two stretcher-bearers toting the corpse of the lately departed Beavertop Baker. Everybody stopped to watch as the grim entourage processed up the street.

Soon after, Cushman arrived to take their statements. And that was the end of the matter as far as he was concerned. An attempted robbery by persons unknown, end of case.

By half past nine, Reece and his partner were loading up the cargo of mail sacks. There were three other passengers, all of whom were full payers.

A travelling drummer who claimed to specialize in medical accoutrements insisted on displaying his latest device for the fast removal of gangrenous limbs. The only female passenger was not impressed. Miss Abigale Barringer's beaky nose sniffed imperiously. A starchy dame in her middle years, she was heading for Grand Falls for the annual conference of the Temperance League.

Last of the trio was the local bank manager bound for Three Forks.

Reece gave him a shifty look of disdain. His breed were not the ex-convict's favourite species of the human race. The notion passed through his mind as to whether this dude and Abner Montague were acquainted. They could even have been in cahoots.

He shrugged off the feeling of

resentment. No good could come of harbouring grudges, at least for now. Maybe once he had dealt with that treacherous backshooter of a partner, he could think about figuring some way of getting even with Montague.

'Time for the stage to leave,' declared the bustling agent, deliberately holding up a pocketwatch for his temporary employees to observe.

'The Butterfield Company takes pride in its punctuality.' He then handed Willard and his partner a shotgun each complete with a box of cartridges. 'And make sure you hand these in to Farley Brooker when you get to Three Forks. He's the agent there. I wired him to expect you.'

'Glad to see you appreciate all the hard work we put in last night to pay for this journey. Not to mention putting our lives on the line.' Willard's mordant smile had no effect on the little guy. 'A fella likes to feel he ain't sponging.'

'Just make sure you complete the rest

of our agreement.' Wally Flood indicated the hardware. 'The mail delivery this week includes a substantial cash transfer that Mr Locket, the bank manager here, is accompanying to Three Forks to hand over to his counterpart.'

A frosty mien soured Reece's face. 'That wouldn't be Abner Montague by any chance would it?'

'You know Mr Montague?' asked Flood innocently.

'We're acquainted,' was all that Reece was prepared to reveal.

Any further discussion was cut short by a gruff retort from a grizzled jasper perched on the bench seat of the coach.

'If'n you varmints have finished chinwagging, we're ready to leave.'

Rooster Bellman was an old army scout who had been paid off after losing a leg during one of Red Cloud's raiding forays. He banged the wooden stump down on the floor of the coach to emphasize his impatience to be off. A hollow sound echoed back.

Unlike the spinster, Bellman had

been particularly taken with the drummer's demonstration of his bone saw.

'If'n the medic at Fort Bozeman had had one of those things, he might have saved me a heap of painful grief,' had been the grumbling conclusion. 'I always know when its gonna rain 'cause this stump gets to throbbing real bad.'

'How's it today then, Rooster?' enquired a smiling Jackdaw.

Bellman cast a thoughtful eye skywards. 'Bet your bottom dollar it'll be another hot and dry one.'

The driver cracked the long bullwhip. The popper on the end snapped as the coach lurched forward. It was only held back by Rooster's wooden leg that was jammed down hard on the brake.

Reece dashed round to the far side and swung up on to the seat beside the grinning driver. In the meantime, Jackdaw had scrambled up over the rear boot locker on to the roof where he had fashioned himself a comfortable spot among the luggage.

Idly lounging against the wall of the

Butterfield office, Geyser Bo Joplin gave no hint that he was avidly listening in to the conversation of the stageline employees. And what he heard brought a restrained smile to the craggy façade.

8

Death Race

'I'd make sure to drop him first.'

The stagecoach had been jouncing along the well-worn trail for a half hour before these first words were uttered. The flat terrain held little of interest. And Reece's thoughts had drifted back over the train of events that had led to his incarceration.

He had no doubts that the bullet lodged in his ribs on that fateful morning of the robbery had been intended as a killing shot. Sam Foley must have mistakenly figured he'd achieved his aim when Reece had fallen to the floor of the bank. Learning that his old buddy was still alive, albeit serving a prison term, must have come as a stunning blow. After all, it was front page headlines throughout the territory.

During his sentence, hardly a day passed when Reece did not rattle his brains figuring out why it had happened. Sure they'd had disagreements, but nothing that would warrant a bullet in the back.

And now Reece Willard was a free man. Free to get his revenge by seeking out the treacherous skunk who had tried to kill him. But before he killed the rotten four-flusher, he wanted to know exactly why Foley had turned on him in such a yellow dog manner.

His rugged features twisted in thought.

So what would a guy do under those circumstances? Reece tried to put himself in Foley's position.

The words were blurted out before he could stop himself.

'What's that you said?' Rooster shouted above the raucous din. The drumming hoofs together with the creak and rattle of the stagecoach made for a constant ear-pummelling cacophony. 'You got to holler like a demented coyote to make yourself heard above this racket.'

Reece was taken by surprise. But he quickly managed to correct his careless outburst. 'I asked how long it would take us to reach Three Forks.'

He would have to be much more heedful in future. The last thing he needed was to alert some sharp jasper to his vindictive designs. Rooster Bellman seemed like a straight-up sort of guy, the type who would sympathize with his intention. There again, he was a loyal company man, and any illicit deed might be condemned outright.

Rooster nodded. He'd heard right this time. 'Keep up this pace and we should make it by around five o'clock tomorrow evening.'

*   *   *

The coach spent that night at the Gallatin Springs relay station which was around the halfway mark. It was a bleak outpost that offered only the most basic of fare. Miss Barringer was offered a hard cot for the night but the men had to make do with straw palliasses in the barn, much to the chagrin of Jeremiah Locket.

Reece took malicious delight in the banker's discomfiture.

Supper was fried fatback and beans liberally sprinkled with sand. But at least the coffee was thick and strong to wash away the rancid taste. Rooster Bellman ate his meal with evident relish, belching loudly with approval. He and the station manager were old scouting buddies. They had much to talk about over a jug of homemade moonshine.

It was towards noon of the following day when the stagecoach approached the only visible outcropping of red sandstone on the otherwise level plateau.

Badger Rock was a remnant from a bygone age. The large chunk of red sandstone had somehow managed to survive the erosive power of the ice sheet. The erratically carved pinacle was the result of wind-blown sand. It acted as a prominent landmark by which travellers were able to navigate their passage across the arid wilderness.

Geyser Bo and his sidekicks were concealed behind the rock's sturdy bulk. The idea of robbing the stage-coach of its valuable cargo would be an added bonus to killing the ex-convict. When he had first proposed the notion, Boise McCabe had viewed it with deep scepticism.

'We ain't road agents, Bo,' he had stressed. 'Our job is to collect rents for Foley and to back him up with muscle. Robbing well-guarded stagecoaches is too risky. Why not wait until it reaches Three Forks. We could easily lure Willard into a trap down one of the back alleys.'

Joplin shot his confederate a sneering look of disdain. The thought of securing a heap of dough was worth the risk as far as he was concerned. And he voiced his contempt for McCabe's uncertainty with vituperative expletives. 'You losing your nerve, Boise? Never figured you for a yellow cur.'

McCabe bristled angrily. His hand strayed to the gun on his hip. 'I ain't no coward,' he snarled. 'And I ain't no durned fool neither.'

The two men faced each other, neither wishing to back down.

It was Dakota who managed to calm the troubled waters.

'No sense arguing among selves,' he posited, stepping between the two men. 'But Dakota agree with Boise. Too much of gamble.'

Joplin huffed, his piercing eyes twitching with rancour. 'If'n you pair of old maids can't stomach robbing a stagecoach, then I'll go it alone. No way am I about to let that amount of dough slip through my fingers.'

He stalked off. A large drink in the Old Moses beckoned to cool his anger. McCabe and the half-breed shrugged, following behind. Joplin was their acknowledged leader. They'd been together for over two years now. Splitting up to go their separate ways was not an option to be relished.

Boise McCabe was a follower, not a leader. He needed somebody to give the orders.

As for the half-breed, Dakota could expect no help from his tribesmen after dallying with the chief's wife. He had been lucky to escape with a whole skin. Now he was an outcast from his own people. Condemned to wander the frontiers of the west, a half-breed scorned by both white and red. Bo Joplin was the only man who had accepted him as he was.

Ten minutes later, it was as if nothing untoward had occurred.

'Glad to see you boys have come to your senses,' Joplin grinned pouring them all a drink. 'Now let's get to planning this robbery and how we're gonna spend all them lovely greenbacks.'

It was Dakota's acute hearing that picked up the rattle of the approaching stagecoach.

'Here in five minutes,' he declared. Only a slight tenseness in the Indian's neck muscles betrayed his unease.

McCabe's anxiety was more visible in the form of sweat dribbling down through the dark stubble of his cheeks. The edges of his mouth twitched as he struggled to maintain an outward show of mettle. This was the first time that any of them had pulled such a stunt. And that included Bo Joplin, even though he had implied that this was not his first such robbery.

'Soon as the coach passes the Rock, we spur out and catch them from the rear,' Joplin reminded his associates. 'That way they get caught by surprise. It will also be harder to hit us if'n they try to shoot back. Now check your pistols are fully loaded.'

The plan had been hatched in the Old Moses. Every contingency to affect a successful outcome had supposedly been covered. That did not give extra confidence to Boise McCabe and his

Sioux confederate. They both merely grunted. The die was cast. There was no backing out now.

Three buzzards circled the probing summit of Badger Rock. Their mournful cawing sent a shiver down Dakota's rigid spine. An ominous portent that heralded bad tidings. Gritting his teeth, he shrugged it off.

As soon as the coach had trundled past Badger Rock, Joplin gave a raucous bellow. 'OK, boys, let's go rob us a stage.'

The three robbers, bandannas over their faces, dug in their spurs. The horses leapt forward. Out on the trail, they thundered after the coach. Pistols drawn they began firing at the heads visible above the luggage on the Concord's roof.

'What the heck . . . ' Rooster ejaculated as a slug buzzed past his right ear. He swung round. 'It's a hold-up!' he shouted.

Slapping the leathers, he elicited a roaring whoop.

'Yaaaahoooo, me beauties!' he hollered. 'Let's show these mangy coyotes what we're made of.' A manic grin split the seamed contours. The old dude actually seemed to be enjoying the challenge.

The long whip cracked as Bellman urged the team of six to greater speed. The pounding rhythm was instantly hiked up.

Reece swung round, planting his knees on the bench seat. The shotgun rested on a leather case. Picking off one of the robbers, he pulled both triggers together. The blast slammed the stock back into his shoulder as the lethal charge was unleashed. But the awkward bouncing of the coach on the rutted trail thwarted his aim. Instead, a bunch of cholla cacti exploded in a welter of green mush.

A bullet plucked at his sleeve. But the searing pain in his arm was ignored as he turned to reload.

In front of Reece, Jackdaw had more luck. His cartridges blew a hole in the chest of Boise McCabe.

The loss of his sidekick was ignored by Joplin whose attention was concentrated on emptying his pistol at the fleeing coach. But replies to the gang's barrage of lead were now coming from inside the coach as well as on top of it.

Jeremiah Locket had no intention of the bank's transfer money being purloined by any low-down thieving critters. The small Colt Lightning that he always carried added to the cacophany but did no damage. Locket's expertise was in the manipulation of money and not gunplay.

Joplin's Smith & Wesson Schofield clicked on to an empty chamber. He immediately stuck it back into the right holster and drew another poking from his gunbelt to continue the fusillade. The lethal volley paid off.

Rooster Bellman had been concentrating on getting increased speed out of his team to the detriment of his safety. He stood up to more effectively brandish the whip and leathers. A bullet struck him in the back. The driver threw up his arms and plunged forward, disappearing under the pounding wheels.

The sudden lurch almost threw Jackdaw off his hazardous perch on the coach roof. He managed to grab a hold of the metal railing. But in doing so was forced to release his hold of the shotgun which vanished over the side.

Reece blasted off three more loads before he struck lucky. Dakota's premonition of disaster had come to fruition. The lethal dose of buckshot punched him off the back of his horse. Clearly, the lucky amulet given to him by a medicine-man to ward off death had lacked a special ingredient. The Indian would be joining his ancestors sooner than expected.

With his gang decimated, Joplin realized that unless he abandoned the attack, he would likely go the same way. Robbing well-guarded stagecoaches was clearly not the simple task that he had envisioned. He dragged his horse off the trail and into the cover offered by a cluster of cottonwoods.

Now he was on his ownsome.

A seething intent, however, still burned in his breast. That durned sidewinder had the luck of the devil on his side. Such a streak could not last for ever. And Joplin was not about to scurry back to Medicine Hat with his tail between his legs. The look on his dust-smeared face hardened. Grief for the loss of his buddies played no part in a burning resolve to make Reece Willard pay for this humiliation with his life.

With a growling shake of the fist, Joplin watched, stoney-faced, as the bolting coach disappeared in a cloud of dust. A cheer from the passengers inside the coach did nothing to soothe his petulant mood.

But all was not hunky-dory with the stagecoach.

Its driver lost, the team of horses had no means of being steered. They had panicked and were now careering along the trail on a death race to destruction. Unless something was done to bring them under control, the coach and its occupants were surely doomed.

The leathers were flapping out of reach. Reece tried stamping his foot on the brake lever, but to no avail. His only option was to jump on to the central linked beams beside which each pair of horses was secured. It was an exceedingly dangerous operation. The slightest miscalculation and he would be thrown under the pounding hoofs.

But there was no other choice.

'You come sit on the bench,' he shouted over his shoulder to Jackdaw. The old-timer scrambled down beside him.

He sensed what was on his partner's mind.

'That's suicide, boy,' he railed. 'One slip and you're finished.'

'If'n I don't, we're all finished.' A fixed resolve indicated that there was no going back now. 'You keep your boot jammed down on that brake lever.'

133

Reece sucked in a deep breath and prepared for the first jump on to the swaying beam. Although never a regular church-goer, he still harboured a belief that a greater power than him was in charge. So he despatched a quick plea for help to the Big Guy upstairs.

Then he launched himself into the dust-laden air.

Scrabbling hands clawed at the leather harnessing, his boots slipping on the jolting beam. But he somehow managed to hang on for dear life.

'Hold on tight! You can do it!' Jackdaw's urgent yell of encouragement registered in his stunned brain. 'They didn't call you the Mule for nothing back in the pen.'

Each hand gripping the traces of the two parallel horses, Reece stepped gingerly forward readying himself for the next leap into the unknown.

This time he was not so lucky. Both legs slipped off the second beam. His body smacked against the left horse's jerking flank. In the blink of an eye, he had slid under the beam and was desperately clinging on upside down, inches from the stamping hoofs and the deadly ground skimming by.

'Aaaaaaggghh!'

The throaty shriek of panic came from Jackdaw. The old guy could only look on, impotent and helpless, willing his young buddy to drag himself back from the brink. Slowly, with jerky movements of arms and legs, Reece managed to edge round and scramble back on to the top of the beam where he lay for the briefest of moments to get his breath back.

But this was no place to linger. Aching muscles had to be pushed to their limits as he clambered back on to his feet. Another deep breath and he was ready for the next and final jump to gain the front horses. This time there was no beam, only a crosspiece which allowed the two leading stallions some measure of freedom.

Balancing precariously on the narrow wooden tongue, he gripped the traces slung around the rumps of the two horses. For a long second he waited for the right moment. Diving forward, searching fingers sought the harnesses slung around the bobbing heads of the stampeding leaders.

Boots desperately clawed for purchase on the broad leather connecting straps. Then with one final heave, he leapt on to the back of the right-hand stallion. The horse appeared not to notice the sudden extra weight. Head down, it ploughed onwards into oblivion.

Reece gripped the bridle and hauled back hard. The bit in the horse's mouth dragged the animal's head up. Its thundering pace faltered. This manoeuvre forced its mate to slow up also.

Yet still they continued their headlong dash. Maintaining pressure on the bridle, Reece gripped the stallion's ears and twisted. The horse whinneyed. And this time its pace noticeably slowed. The whole coach and team shuddered as the entire kit and caboodle stumbled to an untidy halt.

Steam rose in clouds from the lathered flanks, nostrils blowing hard after the perilous flight.

Reece slid off the lead stallion's shiny wet back and staggered away, heaving up the contents of his stomach. After recovering his composure, his gaze fastened on the trail immediately ahead. Another ten feet and disaster would have been unavoidable.

A sharp bend where a cluster of rocky outcrops squeezed the route to a narrow passage would have surely destroyed the coach. He breathed out a sigh of relief as a cheer erupted from those saved from serious injury if not death itself.

Jackdaw leapt off the bench and hurried over. He slapped his partner on the back. 'Boy, that was some stunt you pulled there,' he gurgled. Behind him the three passengers expressed their gratitude in no uncertain terms.

'Anytime you need a fresh limb, sir,' offered the beaming drummer, 'just call on Charles Fothergill and I will arrange a replacement at no cost.'

Reece couldn't restrain a sly chuckle. 'That's mighty decent of you, Mr Fothergill. I can only pray to the good Lord that I never have to call upon your services.'

Jeremiah Locket offered what he considered more practical help. 'You can also seek me out, Mr Willard, if you should require a loan at any time. My bank will give you the most generous of terms.'

The smile instantly dissolved from the unassuming hero's face. He threw a disdainful look towards his partner before standing up and dusting himself down. No further words were spoken as both men went about the business of checking the coach to ensure that it was still trailworthy.

A half hour of soothing whispers were needed to calm the jittery team.

The stoney-faced ex-convict then addressed the banker. 'Perhaps you and Mr Fothergill could walk back up the trail and retrieve the driver's body while me and Jackdaw get the coach ready to continue.'

The blood drained from the faces of the two passengers. Violence and death could not be forgotten so easily. And just to rub salt in the wound, Reece gave them a reminder of that salient truth.

'Keep your eyes peeled just in case that varmint of a bushwacker is still lurking around.'

A half hour later and they were ready to leave.

Rooster Bellman's cadaver was wrapped in a canvas sheet. The macabre package was reverently placed inside the coach. For the first time the old-timer was riding as a passenger. It was unfortunate that he was unable to enjoy the unique experience.

8

The Jackdaw's Croak

The delay on the trail meant that the coach didn't pull into Three Forks until six in the evening.

The Butterfield agent was pacing up and down the boardwalk when it lurched to a halt.

'Where in tarnation have you been until this time?' Farley Brooker bellowed. Then he noticed that the regular driver was absent. 'And who the devil are you, mister? Why ain't Rooster up there? The old coot called in sick again, has he?'

Reece speared the agent with a lowering grimace. He was not prepared to be berated by some jumped-up dogsbody. A menacing retort hissed out, crackling like a bullwhip.

'If'n you take a look inside' — he

slung a thumb back to the coach — 'your sick driver will tell you all about why we were delayed.' A grim smile lacking any humour accompanied the puzzled agent as he went to open the door.

The sight that greeted Brooker's snooty regard took his breath away. All he could do was mumble an abashed request as to what had happened.

'Road agents tried to rob the stage, mister,' snapped Jackdaw. 'But we got the better of them. And Reece here saved the coach from being wrecked when the team broke into a panicking stampede.'

'Yes, sir,' added Miss Barringer, stepping down. 'The man is a hero and deserves a medal.'

'Hear, hear,' agreed Charles Fothergill.

'Well, perhaps you would come inside and fill me in on the details.' Brooker quickly regained his equanimity, acknowledging the good deed with a brisk nod. He then turned a frosty eye towards the young man standing behind him. 'Wipe that smirk off your face, Jarvis,' he rapped, 'and go inform the sheriff and undertaker about this ghastly affair.'

Micah Jarvis quickly hustled away to do his boss's bidding. Although on the way, he had every intention of relaying the comically gruesome events to whomsoever was willing to pay heed. He was certain that there would be no shortage of listeners.

'This way, gentlemen,' the obsequeous toad fawned, ushering the heroes of the hour into his office. 'I am sure that the company will authorize a suitable reward for your brave action.'

The meeting that followed was accompanied by a liberal measure of French brandy and Havana cigars. After relating the course of events, Reece tentatively asked about the potential remuneration.

'When do you figure the dough you hinted at will become available?'

'I will wire the head office in Great Falls first thing in the morning,' replied

Brooker. 'I'm sure they will approve it. Then I can issue a cheque for you to draw the money from the bank.'

'Don't suppose you could make us an advance?' Jackdaw's wheedling tone matched the doe-eyed look of supplication as he appealed to the guy's better nature. 'We ain't got two dimes between us.'

Brooker peered down his beaky snout.

'Guess I could go to ten dollars,' he sniffed, reluctantly extracting a note from his billfold.

'Much obliged,' grinned Jackdaw, snatching the proffered greenback before it could be withdrawn. That would buy them both a good meal plus a bed for the night in a hotel.

At that moment, the sheriff arrived. Mort Harding was a grizzled veteran of the war who still proudly wore the dark blue officer's hat of the Union army. The failed bank robber was unknown to Harding as he had only arrived in Three Forks after the trial.

For the second time, Reece described the occurrence.

'And you say that only one of them jaspers escaped?' the lawman checked.

'He scarpered when his buddies bit the dust,' Jackdaw interrupted, puffing on the large cigar. He then answered what would have been the lawman's next question. 'Didn't get a look at the critter with all the dust flying around.'

'I'll ride out to Badger Rock in the morning and check for sign,' said Harding, while helping himself to a shot of brandy. 'Maybe it'll lead somewhere. Can't promise anything though. Like as not, this varmint will have split the breeze now that his gang has been wiped out.'

★   ★   ★

Following his abysmal failure to join the lawless elite, Bo Joplin had departed the killing ground of Badger Rock with his tail between his legs. He had found a cave empty of bears and varmints to consider his options. Chewing on a stringy rabbit, the flickering tendrils of orange flame threw his shadow across the grey rock walls. Darkness is always apt to depress a man who is down on his luck.

Now a lone brigand, he was seriously considering abandoning Montana. A new gold strike had been discovered in Black Tail Gulch, South Dakota. Maybe he would have better luck there.

The next morning he awoke with the first rays of the sun slanting into the cave entrance. It also brought a fresh outlook.

Why should he let this critter Willard ride roughshod over him? Three of his buddies had been killed. And that needed a suitable hot-leaded response. A pot of strong coffee helped to strengthen his resolve. With the coming of the new day, he set off with a rejuvenated will to get even with ex-convict Reece Willard. And then he would return to Medicine Hat and demand a substantial remuneration for all the trouble the jasper had caused.

The cave was no more than an hour from Three Forks. Drawing close to the town, Joplin's pace slowed to a gentle trot, eyes searching the terrain for signs of life. Having worn a mask, he had no fear of anybody connecting him with the failed robbery of the previous day.

It was when he crested a low rise that Joplin spied a plume of dust rising from the trail a mile ahead. He drew his mount to a halt. Squinting eyes homed in on the distant speck that was causing the disturbance. Within minutes, the blurred form had sharpened into that of a single rider.

Joplin pulled off the trail behind some rocks. And there he sat waiting for the traveller to pass.

Ten minutes later, he heard the steady rhythm of a cantering horse. Peeping out from his hideaway, the brigand was surprised to see that it was a lawman. The tin star glinting in the early morning sunlight announced his profession to the world. And a full sheriff as well.

The guy must be heading for the scene of the robbery to pick up any clues that he could sniff out. Joplin scoffed. It would do him no good. Even if a clear trail had been left for the guy to follow, it would be many hours before he returned to Three Forks. Time enough for Bo Joplin to have his revenge and disappear like the desert wind.

He gave the lawman five minutes before venturing back on to the trail.

A leery smile split the outlaw's face. Having the local starpacker out of town had played right into his hands.

Another half hour passed before the cluster of buildings appeared in a wide amphitheatre below. It was still too early for most folks to be up and about. Nevertheless, ever the cautious operator, Joplin tugged down the wide brim of his battered plainsman to conceal the upper half of his face as he jogged down the main street.

He was sure that nobody would recognize him. But there was no point in pushing his luck.

Probing eyes scanned the wide main street.

None of the few people around paid the newcomer any attention. Just another trail-weary drifter passing through. Joplin knew that somewhere in this berg, Reece Willard would be asking questions concerning the whereabouts of his ex-partner. Foley had insisted that nobody was aware that after the bank robbery, he had fled north over the border into Canada.

But Willard was here and not heading south to California.

Joplin fingered his gun. The time for a confrontation was closing in.

Then his eyes widened. The shambling form of Jackdaw was crossing the street up ahead. The hardcase would have recognized that tousled critter anywhere. He was three blocks down and headed this way.

Here was being offered the perfect

opportunity to take out one of his marks.

Joplin steered his horse over to the same side opposite a dim alleyway. Dismounting, he led the horse into the gloomy portal and tied off before returning to the main street. Casually, he leaned against the wall of a dressmaker's store and watched the old reprobate as he ambled down the street. He was now only one block away.

As the old guy drew level, he gave no hint of having recognized the road agent. Joplin kept his head down to preserve his anonymity.

'Mind taking a look at my old nag, mister?' he grunted from beneath the plainsman. 'He seems to have gone lame and I ain't too good with broncs.'

'Sure thing,' breezed Jackdaw, who was willing to help out. 'I done some blacksmithing while working on a horse ranch down in Colorado. Where is he?'

With a vague gesture, the stranger led the way down the alley.

'I think something is wrong with his

front leg,' said Joplin, edging behind the helpful old-timer.

Jackdaw bent down to lift the indicated leg. 'Could be just a stone stuck in his hoof. Let's take a look see.'

Joplin drew a knife from his boot sheath.

'Can't see nothing wrong here,' Jackdaw said with a frown. He ran a hand down the leg. 'Don't seem to be anything wrong with him at all.'

The knife rose. The macabre glint in the killer's eyes bored into Jackdaw's back.

'You shouldn't ought to have blasted my partner, old man,' Joplin hissed in his ear. 'For that you have to pay the full price.'

Jackdaw's head turned. A shocked expression registered on his wrinkled face. Impulsively, he grabbed for his attacker. But it was too late. Joplin easily shrugged him off. The knife plunged down into his exposed back. Not a sound emerged from the open mouth as he sank to the floor.

So deep was the fatal weapon buried in the dead man's rib cage that Joplin had to use his boot to lever it out. He spat on the blood-stained corpse, wiping the dripping blade on the dead man's shirt.

No remorse for the cowardly act showed on the killer's granite hard features. Indeed, he was well satisfied with the outcome.

Quickly he dragged the lifeless body over to the building on his left and manhandled it beneath the supporting beams. Two empty barrels close by were rolled in front to conceal the odious iniquity. With any luck, it would remain there, undetected, possibly forever. Or until the stink of rotting flesh permeated the store above.

The prissy old maid who ran the dressmaker's would get the shock of her life when she discovered what had caused it. Joplin chuckled at the thought. But he would be well away if that happened.

Just then, a slight movement to his

left caught the killer's eye. He swung round grabbing for his hogleg.

But it was only a black cat. The feline spectator must have witnessed the entire gruesome episode.

'You ain't gonna tell on old Geyser, are you kitty?' Joplin purred exaggerating a wheedling tone. ' 'Cause if'n you are, I'd have to kill you too.' He quickly drew his revolver and aimed it at the tensed-up cat. 'Bang! Bang! You're dead.' He chortled with glee, as the terrified animal scooted off round the corner.

The blithe expression cloaking Joplin's visage instantly disappeared. The next victim on his list was still in town and he would not be so easy to hoodwink.

'Reckon it's gonna have to be a straight bullet in the back for you, Mr High-and-Mighty Willard.'

He peered around to ensure that nothing suspicious remained to indicate that a heinous murder had just taken place. Sauntering casually out of the

152

alley, Joplin ambled down the board-walk to the saloon and planted himself in a chair outside to await developments.

The killer was impatient. He wanted action. The next hour passed with the speed of a desert tortoise and the Geyser was threatening to blow. But there was no sign of Reece Willard.

Levering himself up, Joplin wandered across the street to the hotel. Foley had given him a generous expense allowance. With his three sidekicks removed from the picture, the dough was all his.

So he booked the best room in the house. The fine apartment contained all the luxuries normally denied to a humble bodyguard. There was a connecting bathroom with hot water and the services of a visiting barber, not to mention a complementary drinks cabinet of which he now took full advantage.

A large Scotch burned down his throat.

The leery smirk playing across the

hard contours of his face indicated the brigand's anticipation of his next killing. It was a sweet thought.

And in the blink of an eye Geyser Bo was fast asleep. No remorseful irritants of conscience to disturb his repose.

Had he known that his quarry was at that moment occupying another room at the far end of the corridor, future events might well have turned out differently.

It was the chiming of the clock downstairs in the lobby that awoke him on the stroke of noon.

10

No Luck for Geyser

Reece paused opposite the Rolling Dice. His eyes strayed to the building adjacent to the saloon on its left.

The dance hall was finished and no longer boasted that freshly painted look after seven years. On the other side was the bank. A sour grimace clouded the observer's rugged features. That had not changed except for the fact that its manager had doubtless assumed ownership of the saloon.

He crossed the street and pushed open the door of the Rolling Dice. Searching eyes rapidly adjusted to the gloomy interior as he absorbed the familiar sights and smells. The bartender was different. Charlie Vickers must have moved on. The lilting sounds of a band reached his ears from the adjoining room informing him that the dance hall was in full swing.

Reece ambled up to the bar and ordered a beer.

'Ain't been around here for a spell,' he said, sipping the cold drink. 'What happened to Charlie Vickers?'

'The new owner found out that he had been creaming off the bar profits and pilfering Scotch,' the barman huffed with a disdainful snort intimating that he was above any such chicanery. 'He had the boys kick him out, literally!'

That gave Reece the opportunity to make further enquiries.

'I heard that the previous owner lit out in a hurry.'

'Sure did.'

'What happened?' asked Reece.

'He robbed the bank and shot his partner, then skidaddled,' enthused the barman eager to expand on his knowledge. 'That was over seven years ago. Turns out they'd dug a tunnel from the cellar right beneath where we're standing. And nobody suspected a durned thing.' The guy shook his head in bewilderment. 'Craziest story I ever heard.'

'Any notion where this guy went?' posited Reece, casually wrestling to maintain a blank expression.

'Some say he headed for California.' The barman shrugged. 'But I can't say for sure. What I do know is that his partner survived and ended up in the state pen.'

'Who's running the place now?' asked Reece.

The sharp barman slung a suspicious glance at the stranger. 'You seem mighty interested in something that happened many years ago,' he said.

Reece shrugged off the doubting remark. 'As you said yourself, it's a really weird yarn. Must have been in all the newspapers.'

'You must have been out of the territory for a long while if'n you never heard it,' declared the barman, satisfied with Reece's rejoinder.

'I've come north from Colorado,' he said. 'Hope to stake me a claim in the Beaver Lodge gold strike.'

He didn't want to press the point regarding the current ownership of the Rolling Dice. That would be pushing his luck too far. So he was pleased when the jovial bartender provided the answer without any prompting.

'The bank took over the place and put Frenchie La Belle in charge as manager. She was a dancer here. But she's got a canny head on her shoulders, has Frenchie. Not to mention other personal assets that Abner Montague, the bank manager, was hoping to get acquainted with' — the barman tapped his nose adding with a sly wink — 'if'n you get my drift.'

Reece's whole body stiffened at the mention of his hated adversary's name. But he merely nodded. So Frenchie was in charge of the Rolling Dice. And that odious banker was still no doubt cheating honest citizens. Both revelations needed some digesting.

Montague's continued presence in Three Falls did not surprise him. But learning of Frenchie's association with the skunk had come as a blatantly unwelcome shock. He didn't quite know what to make of that surprising disclosure. It sure wasn't what he had expected to hear.

Reece moved away to the end of the bar to contemplate these stunning revelations. What really stuck in his craw the most, however, was not the fact that Frenchie was running the joint. It was her relationship with that scheming rat. His fist gripped the beer glass, threatening to crack it.

The thought of them together was something he had never contemplated in his wildest dreams. Nor had he expected the outpouring of jealousy that was now wracking his taut frame. He had always figured that she would get it together with Sam Foley. That notion had been stymied following the robbery.

Now this! Maybe if'n it had been

anybody else, he wouldn't have bothered so much. But Montague — that was like a slap in the face.

Reece slung the rest of the beer down his throat and ordered a bottle of whiskey. This needed a hard drink to settle his churned-up emotions. Had he been in love with the dancehall queen all along? Maybe his feelings had been stifled beneath a greedy ambition to make a heap of dough.

Another issue that was bugging him concerned the whereabouts of his current partner. Jackdaw had left the hotel early on. Ostensibly to sniff around, he had hoped to learn something to their advantage. But it was now past noon.

Where in tarnation was the old dude?

He wandered outside and looked up and down the street. Not a sign. Maybe the old-timer had found a bottle and was sleeping off the contents someplace. His thoughts drifted back to the question of Frenchie La Belle.

At the same moment that Reece was

wrestling with sentiments that he found distinctly alien and unsettling, Bo Joplin was stretching out his stiffened muscles. Bottle in hand, he casually looked out the window of his room.

His eyes widened on sighting his hated quarry standing outside the saloon across the street with a bottle in his hand. The guy looked around then went back inside the Rolling Dice.

Geyser grinned. Here was his chance to rub the skunk out and leave town before the sheriff returned.

Buckling on his gunbelt, he removed the sturdy Schofield and checked the gun had a full load. A final slug of whiskey, then he slipped out of the door, turning right towards the back of the hotel. For what he had in mind, Geyser did not want any nosey reception clerk witnessing his movements. The door at the far end of the upper corridor opened on to an empty back lot where his horse was grazing.

Eagle eyes panned the immediate vicinity. Nobody was in sight. He led the animal round to the front and tied off in front of the saloon ready for a quick getaway.

Peeping through the grimy window he could see his adversary nursing a drink at the far end of the bar. A curse rumbled in his throat. The distance was too great for an accurate pistol shot. He would need to get closer.

Pushing open the door he stepped inside the long narrow room. The tinkling of a piano came from the adjoining dance hall. There were few drinkers in the Rolling Dice at that time of day. A couple sitting at the roulette table on the right and a poker game on the left were the only other occupants apart from the lone drinker.

The situation was perfect for what Joplin had in mind. Gun the bastard down and get the hell out of there with no one to foil his plan.

Gimlet eyes narrowed. The gun was palmed. He gently snapped the hammer back to full cock. Nobody heeded the surreptitious manoeuvre.

Joplin's arm rose as he sighted along the barrel, his finger tightening on the trigger.

'To hell you're bound, sucker,' he breathed.

At that very moment, a high-pitched scream cut through the fetid atmosphere.

'Behind you, Reece!'

The warning yell came as the revolver spat lead. A split second for the potential victim to duck down. The bullet buzzed overhead smashing into the mirror behind the bar and shattering it into myriad fragments. Another shot rang out chewing slivers of wood from the bartop, inches from the victim's head.

One splinter sliced through his cheek. The wound drew blood but Reece felt no pain. His whole being was intent on survival, dodging the hail of lead pouring his way.

Reece was bent low, one leg kneeling on the floor while his left hand dragged a table over to cover him. His own weapon replied to the bushwacker's heinous attack. The first shot went wide. But the next lifted Joplin's hat into the air. Reece couldn't resist despatching another bullet to send the plainsman spinning off into a corner of the room.

An exchange of shots followed after which there was a frantic scuffling as both men sought to reload their weapons. The gamblers had already hit the deck, anxious to avoid any stray bullets.

The battle was not going Joplin's way. He had hoped to end it with a single shot. Now he was engaged in an equal contest but where time was not on his side. He had lost the advantage. Better to retire and try again when he could be certain of achieving his terminal objective.

Slowly, he began dragging the table backwards towards the door of the saloon. His whole attention was focussed on reaching the street and escaping. As a result he had failed to observe the bartender creeping up behind him. Too late he saw the shadow of the bulky beer-puller. The sturdy cudgel slammed down on his exposed head.

Joplin keeled over, out for the count.

Gunsmoke drifted in the static air, the reek of cordite thick and heavy as a morbid silence filled the room. Suddenly, a babble of conversation broke out as the customers expressed views as to what had started the fracas.

Reece stumbled to his feet and hurried across to the ambusher.

'Much obliged, barkeep,' he panted. 'I owe you one.'

The portly guy nodded. 'Old faithful here always comes in handy when things get out of hand.' Then he went back behind the bar to serve the extra customers who had entered the saloon to see what all the shooting was about.

Reece turned at the touch of a hand on his shoulder.

'You OK?' came the lilting tones that he had not heard for seven long years.

And there she was, as beautiful as ever. The intervening years had been good to Frenchie La Belle. Red hair cascaded over her bare shoulders like a rampant prairie fire. Reece was lost for words.

Suddenly he felt faint. Watery eyes misted over. The fight had taken a lot out of his still weakened body. The bullet stuck in his ribs ached like the devil. And worrying about Jackdaw hadn't helped either. Then there was the discovery that he had deep feelings for this woman that had lain dormant in his subconscious all this time. Worst of all, however, was learning of her association with one of the dirty skunks that had caused his downfall.

It was all too much. Reece slumped over.

'Hey, Chuck, Pete!' Frenchie called across to her security guards. 'Get this galoot upstairs into my rooms.' The pair of hard-asses rushed across to obey their feisty boss.

Then she turned to address a giant of a man who had been ogling the dancers practising for the evening floor show in the dance hall. She ignored the fact that Goliath ought to have been keeping an eye on the bar. But her trenchant gaze left the hefty jasper in no doubt that he would be on the receiving end of the boss's acid tongue in due course.

'You figure it ain't too much bother to go bring Doc Lawson over to fix this guy up?'

'Sure thing, Miss La Belle,' he gushed. The sarcastic retort was lost on the burly minder. 'What should I do about this critter?' A pudgy thumb indicated the prostrate body of Geyser Bo Joplin.

Frenchie considered for a moment. 'Sling him in the cellar,' she ordered, 'and make sure he's securely tethered.'

It was an hour later when the aging sawbones announced that his patient was just suffering from exhaustion. The cut on his face was superficial. A bandage swathed his head where the cheek had been opened up. The guy's palid complexion, however, was not lost on the medic.

'All this fella needs is to rest up for a few days,' said the doctor. 'Get him to take these pills as and when needed. They're a new line of painkillers if'n he gets a headache. But you might also want to ask him what he's been doing in the slammer for the last few years.'

Doc Lawson was new in Three Forks and had no recollection of the previous saloon owner and his bizarre circumstances. But he could recognize an ex-jailbird when he saw one.

Frenchie merely nodded. She had no intentions of satisfying the medic's curiosity. 'Much obliged for your attention, Doc,' she said, ushering him out. 'Just send me the bill when you're ready.'

A pained grunt found the woman hustling back into her room to tend her patient. Reece's eye flickered open. The first thing he perceived was the concerned frown cloaking the vision of beauty. A searching hand reached up and stroked the soft cheek. Was he in heaven or hell?

'What happened?' he croaked struggling to raise himself.

'You were in a gun fight. Then you collapsed from exhaustion,' Frenchie related, her gentle tones helping to allay the patient's anxieties. 'But you're in good hands now. So rest up and take it easy.' She smiled. Her whole face seemed to light up the dim room. 'Doctor's orders.'

'What happened to the varmint who bushwacked me?'

'He's being held prisoner down in the cellar until Sheriff Harding returns,' replied Frenchie. 'He has a lump the size of duck egg on his head. My barman ain't employed just to serve drinks.'

'I need to question him about why he wants me dead,' Reece emphasized, trying to rise. 'And Jackdaw's disappeared. With this dude in town, I got me a bad feeling.'

'Rest up for a few hours,' the woman

asserted firmly, gently easing the crusty patient back down on to the bed. 'Then we'll think about it.'

Reece accepted the gentle yet firm insistence with a tender smile. But then his lips compressed into a hard line as a more sour thought nudged out the rose-tinted images.

Frenchie instantly picked up on the cooling of the atmosphere.

'Something bothering you, Reece?' she asked.

'Never figured that you'd get it together with a skunk like Abner Montague. He's the reason for me ending up in the pen. Him and the betrayal of a supposedly loyal buddy.'

Frenchie stiffened. 'I ain't as you imply, 'getting it together' with no anyone. Montague is my boss and that's it. He might want a few extras. But it takes two for that sort of liaison. And anyway, why shouldn't I accept employment. A gal has to earn a living. And running your own place is a sight better than being a dancer.'

Her feathers thoroughly ruffled, the woman stood up and moved away. She harboured a suspicion as to why Sam Foley had shot his partner in the back. These were now delivered in subdued tones.

'I received wires from him some months after he disappeared pleading with me to join him. He even asked me to marry him,' she murmured while pacing up and down the room. 'But I never replied. Perhaps I should have refused all the presents he showered on me before all this blew up. But I was flattered. All guys had ever wanted before was . . . you know?'

There was no need to elaborate further.

'I knew he was smitten,' replied the stunned man, 'but I never gave him cause to figure my association with you was anything but professional.'

'If'n you'd taken the hint back then, you'd have known that it wasn't Sam I was keen on.' Frenchie's snappy retort was waspish and barbed. She stopped, head lowered, tears dribbling down her cheeks as the fire was extinguished. 'Why in tarnation did you think I blew up after you'd suggested that I could pose naked for that bar-room painting? I was hoping you thought much more of me than that.'

Her innermost feelings revealed, Frenchie sat down. A lace handkerchief dabbed at her smudged make-up.

Reece was dumbfounded. The benumbed look was replaced by one intended to convey a thousand regrets.

'Perhaps if'n I'd read the signs, things would have been different. Although knowing Sam, I doubt it. But I never guessed!' he exclaimed impotently. 'Why didn't you tell me how you felt?'

'It ain't for a gal to reveal how she feels,' Frenchie railed. 'You should have taken the numerous hints that were dropped. But no. Reece Willard was much too involved with the saloon and making his fortune to give poor little me a second glance.'

'I know that now,' Reece pleaded. A

hand reached out and took hers. 'I was stupid and selfish.' He gulped, doleful eyes exhorting this winsome creature to extend him an olive branch. 'Is there any chance for us now?'

In an instant she was in his arms.

'You don't know how long I've waited for you to say that,' she purred. They kissed. It was intensely passionate. An ardent exhortation of restrained feelings too long dormant and now bursting forth.

11

A Shock for Willard

It was a knock on the door that brought Reece Willard back to the reality of Three Forks and his quest for vengeance. Until that was appeased, he could not move forward.

Gently yet firmly he prised himself free of the woman's clinging embrace.

The summons went unanswered.

'Did those wires give any hint as to where Sam had set down?' Reece enquired.

Frenchie shook her head. 'They all came from a central telegraph box number of a lawyer in Denver, Colorado. He must have hired the guy to help conceal his tracks.'

'So we still have no idea where the skunk is lurking,' growled Reece in frustration.

There was a second knock on the door.

'Who is it?' Frenchie snapped.

'It's me, Goliath,' came the gruff response. 'That critter in the cellar has come round.'

'I'll be down in ten minutes after I've finished these accounts,' Frenchie called back.

She winked at Reece, reluctantly pulling away from the insistent embrace. Quickly smoothing down her ruffled hair and tidying her make-up, she murmured, 'So where do we go from here?'

That was when Reece informed his beloved about his grim objective to hunt down Sam Foley. On hearing this, she implored him to think again.

What use could be served in harbouring such a callous grudge? The past was gone. Seeking vengeance could only end in him being hunted down by the forces of law and order. How could he consider such action when they had only just found each other?

Only when Reece had revealed the

true nature of the robbery and the heinous part played by Abner Montague could she fully understand his motives.

The reason for the robbery was well known. It had all come out during the trial. What had remained in the shadows was the nature of the original contract. Abner Montague had ensured that only the bogus document saw the light of day.

'And I am convinced that the murdering varmint downstairs in the cellar has the answer to where Sam is hiding out,' Reece concluded, swinging his legs off the bed. 'Why else would he have tried to bushwack me? Don't make no sense. Jackdaw and me ain't got a plugged nickel between us.' He went on to reveal the attempt on his life in the Butte livery stable. 'And I'm going to make durned sure he spills the beans. Then once Sam has paid his dues, I'm coming back for Montague.'

Frenchie laid a restraining hand on his arm.

'If'n I go along with your madcap scheme,' the woman expressed with vigour, 'you must promise to obtain justice through the official legal process. I want nothing to do with a man who chooses to ride the owlhooter trail.' Frenchie fixed him with a sombre regard. 'Promise me!' she demanded.

He returned the woman's ardent gaze. 'I promise to give the guy every chance to admit his guilt and surrender himself to the law.' He paused offering an equally serious response. 'But if'n either of these galoots chooses to resist, I have every intention of defending myself. And that might lead to gunplay.'

That was as much as Frenchie La Belle could expect. She reluctantly nodded her consent.

As they made to leave the room to interrogate the captive, Reece caught Frenchie's arm and drew her back.

'Best that you aren't a witness to this,' he said. 'I might have to use force to encourage the skunk to talk.'

Frenchie balked at the notion that

she was a strait-laced dame. 'I ain't no milksop, fella,' she remonstrated vigorously. 'It takes a tough skin to run a place like the Rolling Dice. And mine is like steer leather.'

'Didn't feel like that to me a moment back.' Reece gave her a warm smile following it up with another torrid kiss. Her stiff resolve melted away like hot butter. Then with a more serious disposition he added, 'I wouldn't want any gal of mine seeing her man playing the part of an evil sadist. But that might be the only way to dig out the information I'm certain he is holding.'

Frenchie responded with a nod of understanding. No more was said as she stepped away, watching as he accompanied the giant Goliath down into the bowels of the saloon's macabre cellar.

It was a somewhat unnerving experience knowing the circumstances of his last visit to the underground room.

A flickering oil lamp revealed the tethered captive. Behind him, the entrance to the tunnel had been filled in and bars placed across the cemented outline. Otherwise, the place did not appear any different.

Geyser Bo eyed his visitors with trepidation. All the cocksure arrogance had disappeared. Only a sorry excuse for a human being remained. But Reece felt no sympathy for the man who had tried to kill him.

The tethered man summoned up a surly grimace. The twisted mouth was intended to convey that he was not yet beaten.

It was a forlorn hope.

Without so much as a hint of warning, Reece slammed a bunched fist into the varmint's sneering visage. Such was the force of the blow that Joplin and the chair upon which he was secured went crashing into the wall.

Goliath was well used to dealing with hardcases. But this took him completely by surprise. It did, however, earn the bodyguard's instant respect.

'Man!' he exclaimed in astonishment.

'You sure don't mess around, fella.'

Reece ignored the compliment. His whole attention was focussed on the cowering form on the dirt floor of the cellar.

'Get him up!' he ordered with a snarl, while rubbing his skinned fist with meaningful intent. Geyser was left in no doubt that there was much more of the same to come if'n he didn't spill the beans.

Goliath obeyed the snappy command without any argument. He recognized leadership qualities and responded accordingly.

'Now, mister, let's get down to business,' rasped the ex-convict. His fists lifted ready to deliver more of the same punishment, should it be required. 'What's your name and who sent you to rub me out?'

Joplin returned the probing glare. Blood dribbled down his stubbled chin from the mashed upper lip. He spit out a broken tooth. But he wasn't about to surrender the truth, knowing it was a sure route to his own necktie party on the gallows.

'The name is Geyser Bo Joplin,' the killer drawled out. 'You killed my brother down in Deadwood. I've been on your trail for the last six months.'

Another fist shot out. This time it grabbed the tethered man by the throat and shook him roughly like a rag doll.

'You're a lying bastard,' shouted Reece, his quivering snout no more than an inch from that of the prisoner. 'I've only just been released from the pen. So how could I have been in Deadwood? Now tell me the truth before I beat it out of you.'

'It is the truth,' gurgled Joplin, too late realizing his error. 'Or I thought it was. Maybe I made a mistake. You sure fit the description I was given.'

Reece took a step back. His mind was in a quandary. Was the guy just a lone avenging angel seeking redress, just like himself?

He tried again. 'What have you done with my buddy? An old-timer called

Jackdaw. He set out early this morning and hasn't been seen since.'

Joplin shrugged, a pained expression of innocence on his face. 'Don't know nothing about that. I only just rode in. Saw you in the saloon and just started shooting.'

The door of the cellar opened and one of the other minder's called down.

'Mr Willard?'

'Yeah?'

'The boss wants you upstairs straight away,' said the hidden voice. 'She has some important news that you should hear.'

Reece nodded to Goliath to keep an eye on the prisoner while he was away.

Once in Frenchie's private apartment, he could see immediately that the news she had to impart was not good.

'Your friend Jackdaw has been found,' she uttered in a dolorous voice. She paused, breathing deeply before continuing. 'There ain't no easy way to say this. But I'm afraid he's dead. Stabbed in the back. A dog was seen sniffing at the corpse. It had been pushed under the dressmaking shop.'

Reece's head dropped on to his chest. He desperately tried to hold back the tears. The old-timer had become a part of his life. His good sense and ready wit would be sorely missed. Without thinking, he reached for the bottle of whiskey on a table and tipped a liberal slug down his throat.

'This was found clutched in his hand.' Frenchie handed Reece a silver button. She couldn't help but notice his skinned knuckles. But made no comment. 'Looks like it came from a vest. Find that and you've found your killer.'

'And I reckon I know exactly where it is,' Reece snarled, imbibing another belt. A finger jabbed downwards in the direction of the cellar. Without uttering another word he slammed out of the room, hustling down to confront the killer of his erstwhile partner.

Straight away he grabbed Joplin's vest and examined the buttons.

'What in thunder are you doing?'

complained the killer.

'Recognize this?' Reece shouted, pushing the button under his nose. 'My buddy must have torn it off'n your vest before you knifed him. Then you came after me figuring that I'd be just as easy to remove.' A red mist enveloped Reece's senses. He lashed out at the tethered man. Blood spouted from the mashed proboscis.

Goliath was forced to step in to prevent another killing. He dragged Reece off. 'Carry on like that,' he warned, 'and you'll end up joining this varmint on the gallows. Mort Harding has no time for jaspers that take the law into their own hands.'

'OK, OK, I get your drift,' Reece acknowledged trying ineffectually to break free of the minder's iron grip. 'Just let me ask him one more question, then I'll let you march him over to jail.'

The hard-nosed tough nodded, gingerly releasing his grief-stricken associate.

'Why should I help you?' Joplin

croaked through his swollen mouth. 'I'm gonna swing anyway.'

Reece speared him with a malevolent look of hatred. He didn't speak until his racing heart had slowed to a gentle plod, his temper had calmed, and his thoughts were composed.

A nod of agreement followed the killer's assumption.

'Yeah, buddy. You're going down on a charge of murder,' Reece iterated, his voice wavering with the intense emotion that was coursing through his body. 'Ain't nothing more certain this side of Judgement Day. It's a hangman's rope for sure . . . '

He paused for effect. A thin smile was meant to strike terror into the cringing braggart. He was pleased to observe that it was working.

'Unless that is, somebody informs the judge that you've co-operated with the law in trying to put things right.'

Another brief rest followed. This time it was an inner struggle against all his instincts to send this rat to hell. It also allowed the notion to penetrate the killer's bruised and battered frame.

'But I'd force myself to do it, if'n you were to see sense and answer my questions. Seems to me that you have a heap to gain and nothing to lose. Just make sure it's the whole goddamned truth.'

Joplin knew that this was his only chance to avoid a neck stretching. Sure, he would get a heavy prison term, but just like this guy, at some point he'd get out. Then he'd come looking for him and finish the job properly. That thought brought a greasy smirk to his bruised and battered face. Reece assumed it was a resigned look of collaboration.

'So what d'you want to know?' Joplin grunted, peering through an eye that was rapidly closing.

'Who sent you to rub me out . . . and where can I find him?' Reece snapped.

'Sam Foley paid me to check that you headed for California after being released from the pen.' Joplin paused to get his breath. He winced as a spasm of pain wracked his body. 'I wasn't to do anything unless you headed for Three Forks. Don't ask me what his game is. I'm just the hired help paid to do a job.'

'Where is he skulking now?' pressed Reece impatiently.

'Over the border in Canada,' replied the now thoroughly cowed captive. 'He's set up another saloon in Medicine Hat.'

That was all Reece needed to know.

Without another word, he hustled back up the steps into the main body of the saloon, then ran up the broad staircase to Frenchie's quarters.

'Any success?' enquired the anxious saloon madam.

'Foley has set up in Medicine Hat in Canada,' he clarified with a grim smile that lacked any semblance of humour. 'The sooner I hit the trail, the sooner I can be back here to challenge Montague.'

'And no terminal gunplay!' stressed Frenchie gripping his arm firmly to emphasize her determination. 'Remember that you promised to let the law handle this in the proper way.'

'Don't worry,' Reece assured her. 'I'll do things according to the book . . . providing others involved don't force the issue. And even if there's nothing to prove that Montague is a cheat and a thief, he'll know that I'll be sitting on his tail, watching his every move.'

Content with her new man's pledge of propriety, Frenchie drew him close. They clung together knowing that Reece was entering on a tenuous quest of which the eventual outcome was far from certain.

He kissed her with a fiery passion that was spine-tingling. Neither wanted the dreamlike euphoria to end. But Reece knew that for its continuation, he needed to confront Sam Foley. Hearing the grim truth concerning the deadly act of cowardice from the varmint's own lips was the only way that the unwholesome past could finally be laid to rest.

Then he would kill him.

This latter resolution, however, was not for Frenchie's ears.

After leaving the saloon, Reece went directly to see Farley Brooker at the Butterfield stage office.

He got straight down to business. 'Has the approval of that reward come through?' he rasped.

The agent pushed a cheque across the desk. 'Only just filled it out,' replied the agent. 'You can cash it any time.'

Reece's terse demeanour softened when he saw that the amount was for two hundred dollars, double what he had expected.

'Much obliged for your co-operation, Mr Brooker,' he muttered in a more concilatory tone. 'Some of this will give poor old Jackdaw a good send-off.'

'I was sorry to hear about your partner.' The agent appeared to be genuinely sorry.

Out on the street, Reece's features tightened. His gaze rested on the bank's stolid exterior, his thoughts working out how to deal with the imminent possibility of coming face to face with the despised swindler. Heavy feet crossed the street. Up on the boardwalk, he paused outside the bank, a hand resting on the door handle.

Brushing a bead of sweat from his brow, the ex-convict pushed open the door and entered the cloistered interior. Hat pulled down, he recognized two of the tellers. They had changed little during the intervening years. But Reece was confident he would not be recognized. Prison ages a man. He was not the same person who had been shot down seven years before.

Erring on the side of caution, he chose a new teller to cash his cheque.

That was when the door of the manager's office opened. And there he stood. Abner Montague peered over his steel-rimmed spectacles, the beaky snout twitching with a haughty sniff. His gaze panned the customers, finally coming to rest on the man at the end of the counter.

Their eyes met as Reece pushed back his hat. His face was in full view. For a brief second the banker frowned. Then full recognition dawned.

His mouth dropped open, blood draining from the pasty features. He just stood there, unable to move, rivetted to the spot. Beady eyes locked on to his nemesis in a hypnotic trance.

Reece's whole being screamed out to dive over the counter and throttle this odious toad. But he somehow managed to control his inherent instincts. There was no hint of the anger seething within the craggy façade. The flat regard, cold and devoid of any emotive reaction, was all the more chilling in its effect.

Montague grabbed at the door frame to steady himself. The shock of being confronted by his ignominious past in such a manner had caught him completely off guard. The banker knew that Willard had been released. But he was confident of being in the clear. After all, it was his bank that had been robbed. The law was on his side. And there was no evidence to connect him with the felonious acquisition of the Rolling Dice.

If the culprit returned threatening retribution, Abner Montague considered himself as more than capable of dealing with any fractious outbursts. But Willard's cool demeanour had totally unnerved him.

Did the guy know something? Was he planning to ride roughshod over the meaning of law and order?

Still maintaining eye contact with the bank manager, Reece scooped up the pile of greenbacks, pushed them into his pocket and left the bank.

Montague was left dabbing his damp forehead in a nervous funk. He retired to his office. Locking the door, he grabbed a decanter of Scotch and gulped down a liberal measure direct from the neck.

Reece spent the next hour kitting himself out for the trek north to Medicine Hat. He needed to hire a tough saddle pony and pack mule plus supplies for the two-week trek.

He had not expected to see Frenchie again until his return.

But she was there, on the steps of the boardwalk outside the Rolling Dice as he rode past. He drew to a halt, but remained in the saddle. Frenchie stepped down into the rutted street. She gripped his hand. His own came across and gently stroked her face. Their eyes met.

The meeting was brief. No words were uttered. None were needed.

Then he nudged the horse back into motion. The woman followed his progress until he disappeared from view. A single teardrop rolled down her cheek. Casually brushed away, Frenchie La Belle quickly reasserted the hard-faced, no-nonsense image expected from a woman in her position.

12

Medicine Hat

Ten days after leaving Three Forks, Reece found himself on the edge of Medicine Hat. Black clouds scudded by overhead, heralding an impending storm. The darkly forbidding sight matched Reece Willard's mood.

The journey north had been uneventful.

His arrival came as a surprise. Reece concluded that he must have crossed the border three days previously. But there had been nothing to indicate that he was now in Canada. The last two days had been easy going over flat lush grasslands that were ideal for the raising of beef cattle. Medicine Hat had grown up on a narrow crossing point of the Saskatchewan River. It was perfectly placed for catering to the needs of local ranchers.

Sam Foley had chosen well. There was money to be made in a place like this. And Reece was certain that his erstwhile partner would have taken full advantage of such a bonanza.

These casual musings were now roughly pushed aside. The sooner his business here was over the sooner he could start life afresh.

He peered at the signboard for Medicine Hat. The faded lettering informed him that the town had an elevation of 2576 feet and a population of 524.

A twisted grimace creased the saturnine visage. Soon, that number would be reduced by one.

Now that he was finally about to confront the back-shooting skunk, Reece could feel a tightness in his guts. He had been building up to this moment for so long that it had overshadowed all else.

That was until his blinkered eyes had been opened to the possibilities of a new life with Frenchie. He tried to thrust her radiant vision from his mind. For now, his whole being had to be focussed on the imminent showdown.

He nudged the horse forward. Searching eyes panned the main street. Then he saw it.

The Dice Roll!

It had to be Foley's place. The varmint had even adopted a similar name to his old saloon. It felt like a kick in the teeth. Reece growled. Veering over to the far side of the street but two blocks down, he dismounted and tied off.

A grubby-looking kid was sitting on the ground playing with an equally down-at-heel mutt.

'You want to earn yourself a nickel?' Reece asked the kid.

The boy shrugged. 'Depends what I have to do?' he replied.

'Watch my gear and tell me who owns the saloon over the street.'

The boy considered the proposed task.

'A nickel buys you the name of the dude who runs the Dice Roll.' The astute kid extended an open palm. Reece flicked the coin into the air but caught it before the kid could grab hold.

'And the other job?' he said.

'Now I reckon that will take up a lot more of my time so it'll cost you a dollar,' smirked the youngster, stroking the dog.

'A dollar for both, and that's final.' Reece held his face in a deadpan regard waiting for the kid to agree.

'A deal,' came back the immediate response. The boy had been expecting half that amount. A dollar bill floated in the still air which he instantly snatched and pushed into his pocket.

'So who owns the Dice Roll?' rapped the stranger, whose manner was no longer the easy-going pushover of seconds before.

'Fella by the name of Sam Foley,' relayed the boy. 'But he likes to be known as Dandy Sam. You know this guy, mister?'

'You're being paid to guard my stuff, kid, not ask fool questions,' snarled Reece. 'Just make sure you keep it safe else I'll cut your ears off.'

'S-sure, m-mister,' stammered the thoroughly chastened urchin. 'I didn't mean no harm.'

The tough stranger's face relaxed. He had no wish to antagonize the kid. 'Do the job properly and there'll be a bonus in it for you,' he added, stepping down into the street.

'In that case,' the boy called after him, 'you ain't gonna find him over there today.' Reece swung round waiting for the kid to continue. 'He stays home on Wednesday.'

'And where's that?' he rasped, trying to curb his impatience with this street-wise vagrant.

The kid aimed a grubby finger towards the eastern end of the town. 'Dandy Sam has a smart place on the edge of town. He lives there with his housekeeper.' The kid uttered a lewd chuckle. 'That's what he calls her anyway. There's also a Chinese cook called Lee Fong. You can't miss it. The front door has a giant ace of spades painted on it.'

'You seem mighty well informed, boy,' observed the wary stranger.

'It pays to always keep your eyes and ears open,' grinned the kid. 'You never know when it will pay off.'

Reece returned the wry smirk. This news was better than Reece could have hoped for. Now he did not have to confront the traitor where his body-guards were close at hand. Ambling up the street in the direction indicated, he soon passed beyond the commercial heart of Medicine Hat into a residential zone.

He stopped at a crossroads. To the left lay an amalgam of untidy shacks and tents. The more prosperous citizens were concentrated to the right along a gradually rising street called Nob Hill. He had no doubts that this was where he would find Sam Foley.

The house was at the top of the hill.

And a more imposing edifice he could not have imagined. The black ace of spades stood out starkly against the brilliant white of the door. Ornately carved wooden porticos graced the elegant structure that far outshone any of its neighbours.

Reece stopped to gaze at the building. A gurgle of anger threatened to erupt in his throat. All paid for with his share of the dough.

Concealing himself behind a parked wagon, he gritted his teeth. This varmint had been living the high life while his bushwacked partner was strugging to survive in the hell hole of Butte Penitentiary. Fists blanched as a mist of hatred urged him to go in there with all guns blazing and to hell with the consequences.

Then a more reasoned set of deliberations took control.

He slipped down a narrow passage between the houses, circling round to emerge at the rear of Foley's property. A man was on the back porch. He was reclining in a chair gently rocking to and fro. The concealed watcher's heart skipped a beat. Could it be Foley?

Then a small guy came out of the back door. It was Lee Fong. The Chinaman's appearance was unmistakable. He set down a bottle and glass on a tray before bowing and disappearing back into the house. Reece stared hard at his foe. Gimlet eyes drilled into the guy who was totally unaware that his time on this earth was rapidy drawing to a close.

Foley poured himself a drink and sipped it. A snarl rumbled in the avenger's throat. The rat didn't appear to have a care in the world. Well that is sure going to change, Reece thought. He peered around to make certain he was not being eyeballed.

Luckily, the more wealthy citizens of Medicine Hat appeared to relish their privacy. High fences encircled the properties preventing snoopers from overlooking the activities within. It also meant that none of the neighbours would interfere with his plans.

Here was the perfect opportunity to confront the bastard head on. Reece wanted to see the fear plastered across that unctious façade. He wanted the backshooter to know that his end was nigh, and there was nothing he could do to prevent it.

Before he made his move, however, Reece needed to know that he would not be disturbed. The Chinese cook was inside the house. But where was the housekeeper? Quickly he returned to the front of the house. Strolling unconcernedly up the garden path he knocked on the door.

A brief shuffling inside and the door swung open.

'Yes, sir?' enquired the cook in a melodic high-pitched twang. 'Can I help . . . ' He never got to finish the sentence. Reece pushed him back inside jamming the barrel of his pistol into the little guy's ear.

'Not a sound or you're dead, understand?' growled the intruder.

The cook nodded. His bulging eyes flickered in terror.

'Now where's the housekeeper hiding herself?'

'Miss Charnley has gone to Moose Jaw to visit sister,' gabbled the little man, his whole body trembling.

'And when will she be back?'

'Not for another two days.'

'This just gets better and better,' Reece muttered to himself. He quickly scanned the entrance hall. There was a broom cupboard on the far side. Ushering the cook over, he pushed him inside. 'I don't figure you need telling not to make any noise,' he hissed in the Chinaman's ear.

Lee Fong shook his head vigorously as the door closed on him. Reece turned the key in the lock, removed it and tossed it into a corner.

Now for you, Dandy Sam Foley!

At the back of the house, Reece peered out of the net-covered window. A nod of satisfaction creased the hardened contours. A blank wall overlooked Foley's property. No chance of any prying eyes observing the imminent showdown. Reece's hand gripped the handle of the door leading out on to the rear veranda.

Now that the moment of truth had arrived, he felt a chilling sense of destiny rippling through his taut frame. The culmination of years building up to this one moment was all now converged into a single dedicated aim. All else had paled into insignificance as he opened the door and stepped out.

A tense thumb curled around the Remington's hammer, the barrel swinging towards the reposing figure. Reece scowled. There he was, enjoying the afternoon sunshine with not a care in the world, secure in the notion that his nemesis had been removed from the picture.

Well that was about to change.

The man turned. Even though Reece had made not a sound when closing the door, Foley had heard him. There was certainly nothing wrong with the jasper's hearing.

That was when Reece assimilated his first shock. Sam Foley had aged dramatically during the intervening seven years. His hair was now almost white, his face drawn and pale. The varmint's girth had also spread. None of the cocksure arrogance of his past life remained. In fact, the critter was a mere shadow of his former self.

'That you, Fong?' came the guttural response. 'I hope them cookies are fresh out of the oven.'

The guy's appearance had more than altered but his distinctive Texan drawl was still the same. That was when Reece was hit by a second shock. Foley was staring right at him, yet not a muscle had moved in the guy's face. Surely his old partner must recognize him. Was this visit expected? Maybe Joplin had already sent word that he was on his way.

'Well?' questioned Foley. 'Ain't like you to be so tongue-tied. I normally can't stop you yammering on,' Foley scoffed. 'Don't tell me you've gone and burnt the cookies.'

Reece could only stand and stare as the stark truth dawned. And it slammed into him with the power of a runaway locomotive. For a brief moment, he was indeed lost for words.

13

A Snake With No Bite

Dandy Sam Foley was . . . *blind*!

'Who is that?' A hint of consternation infected the tight query. 'You ain't Lee Fong.' Foley made to rise.

'It's me, Sam.'

The plain statement was delivered in a flat monotone, such was the intruder's sense of bewilderment.

For a brief moment, Foley's brain searched to identify that voice. Then he was likewise jolted by the blunt shock of recognition.

'Reece!' exclaimed Foley, slumping back into his seat. He swallowed nervously. His breathing increased rapidy. But still his solicitude was for the missing Chinaman. 'What have you done with my cook?'

'Don't worry,' Reece replied, having

recovered his equanimity. 'He's only locked in the broom cupboard.' For the moment all thoughts of revenge had been shelved. 'When did this happen?'

'The loss of sight?' Foley didn't wait for a reply. 'It started some months back. Don't matter how it happened. But it's only this last week that it's gotten really bad. I can still make out a blurred form.' A lacklustre gaze was turned on this ghost from Foley's past. 'I can see you standing there. But there's no way that I would have known it was you.'

'How have you managed?'

'It's not been easy,' came back the doleful response. 'But I get by with the help of Fong and my housekeeper.'

With hard-boiled toughs like those sent to get rid of him on the payroll, Reece knew that his old buddy could not have retained their respect had they been aware of his affliction.

'The Chinaman said she was visiting her sister.'

'That's the story I've put about,'

Foley replied, pouring his old buddy a drink. Reece accepted it. He needed a strong belt to calm his nerves following the mind-boggling encounter. 'Truth is, Melinda has gone to Moose Jaw to find a buyer for the saloon and house. I figured it was time to quit this game and settle down some place else.'

'She has to be something special, more than just a housekeeper,' Reece blurted out, trying to hide his confusion. 'You and she must be close to give her that kind of trust.'

'Guess we are at that.' A dreamy cast played over the blind man's face. 'Fact is, I've fallen in love. And she feels the same. So far I've managed the business side of things with the aid of some strong eyeglasses. But with my sight almost gone, selling up is the only option.'

That was when the avenger's reason for coming to Medicine Hat jumped back into focus. It was a stark reminder of the mission of retribution which he had vowed to complete. Enough of this sentimental hogwash. Reece shrugged off any notion of amnesty that he might have been harbouring. A harsh grating replaced the recent tone of disquieting concern.

'So you reckoned that with me removed from the scene, you could just disappear into the wide blue yonder with your lady love.' The gun swung to cover the Judas. 'Well the varmints you sent to rub me out are now worm fodder, not me.'

The final showdown had arrived. But before he pulled the trigger, there were issues that needed resolving.

'We were once friends as well as partners, Sam.' The sound emerging from Reece Willard's throat was cracked with emotion. A mixture of virulent anger and mawkish regret that was difficult to assimilate. 'How could you have gunned me down in the back and then left me for dead?' His head fell forward, the gun hand drooping. 'It just don't make no sense.'

'I thought you were after taking

Frenchie off'n me,' Foley hurried on, hoping to placate his old partner. 'You knew how smitten I was. I even wired her after I settled down here to come and join me.'

'Yeah, she told me about that,' Reece interjected acidly.

'You've been in touch?'

'She's managing the Rolling Dice now.' Reece went on to explain the circumstances of his meeting with the dance hall queen and how it was towards him that she had plighted her troth. 'But when we were running the place, I had no designs on her at all. Didn't have the slightest suspicion how she felt. Frenchie was your gal far as I was concerned. My sole aim in those days was just to make a heap of dough.'

A barbed edge jarred the conflab back to the blunt reality of the face-off.

'But you went and blew all that apart with a bullet in the back.' Again the gun lifted. 'That was the coward's way out. Then you sent a bunch of rabid dogs to ambush me after my release. Trouble was, they got my new partner instead.' There was a catch in the speaker's voice as he recalled his recent associate. 'Jackdaw might have trod the wrong side of the law all his life, but he was a loyal buddy, which is more than can be said for some.'

'Joplin wasn't meant to gun you down,' Foley iterated forcefully. 'I told him to let me know if'n you headed this way. That was all.' The blind man stood up, his sightless gaze imploring the avenger to show mercy. 'I figured I could maybe make amends somehow. He must have reckoned that I'd pay a big bonus to have you removed for keeps.'

Reece dismissed his old buddy's attempt to wheedle out of his treachery.

'And I'm durned sure the bastard would have gotten one had he succeeded,' Reece growled out. 'But he failed. It's him and his low-life rats that are stoking the fires of hell instead.' There was a pause in the flow of invective. 'Now it's your turn.'

Time stood still on the veranda. Then, the sharp click of a hammer drawn back told Sam Foley that his time on this earth was fast disappearing. His next comment, maybe his epitaph, was measured and deliberate. Foley squared his shoulders, drawing himself up and facing his nemesis.

'You're right to call me a yellow dog,' he muttered, barely above a whisper. 'And I did consider how much better life would be not having to continually look over my shoulder, waiting for you to come a-calling . . . '

Reece butted in with a sneering reposte. 'Well now I'm here, ready to square the account.'

Foley ignored the interruption. Things needed saying which now came tumbling out like a flash flood. Again he tried to persuade his old confederate that he truly had repented of his cowardly actions. The whole issue was a nightmare that had haunted him ever since.

'I always regretted what happened,'

he continued. 'I knew you'd come after me once you'd been released. But I thought that I could maybe talk you round.'

Foley paused to draw breath and compose himself.

'Once my finger had pulled the trigger, there was no going back. I owed more dough than you knew about back then. It wasn't just the Rolling Dice. I'd also taken out a loan for a gold mine. But it had proved worthless. And then there was me thinking you were after Frenchie. It was all too much. I wasn't thinking straight. Getting my dirty hands on all that money in the safe seemed the only way out.'

Breathing deep, Foley wiped the sweat from his brow. Reliving the sordid actions of his past was tough going.

'The whole thing has been like a ball and chain round my neck ever since. And now that I've lost my sight, life ain't worth a blamed cuss. Another week and the specialist says that everything will be black as night.' He held out his arms in surrender.

'So, go ahead. Shoot! You'll be doing me a big favour.'

Reece grunted. His finger tightened on the trigger. But those blank, dead eyes staring back made him hesitate. The lantern jaw tightened as the avenger willed himself to complete the task upon which he had embarked.

It was no use. He couldn't do it.

Reece Willard was no hard-ass killer. How could he gun down a helpless man in cold blood? Releasing the hammer, the gun was returned to its holster.

'You mean that you ain't . . . ?'

'Reckon you've suffered enough for the both of us,' Reece assured the blighted man. 'Don't think I could have done it anyway. Shooting a man down when he can't defend himself ain't for the likes of me.'

'After me doing just that, and making you serve seven years of hell, don't I deserve to die for it?' protested Foley.

'But as you said yourslf, you were in desperate straits. And your mind was all

215

in a flap. Harbouring a grudge all this time has soured my mind as well. It's time to put the past behind us and move on with a clean slate.'

Sam Foley uttered a potent sigh of relief when he knew that his life had been spared. 'I never really wanted to die. Not now that I've found Melinda. We've been together for six months. She's been a tower of strength since my affliction worsened. I figured when she found out, that would be the end. But she's vowed to stand by me. Ain't that something, old buddy?'

'Sure is, Sam. You're a lucky guy. I'll be leaving now. Hope things turn out OK for the two of you.'

'I appreciate your understanding, Reece. And I can repay you in the one sure way that will make that wish possible.'

Reece frowned. 'What you driving at, Sam?' he enquired.

Foley delved into his jacket and pulled out a large key.

'Take this and open the safe in the

front room,' he said handing over the key. 'Inside you'll find a large brown envelope. I think that you'll find the contents rather interesting.'

The sly smirk intrigued Reece. But he made no further comment as he headed back inside the house. Five minutes later he returned with the envelope. He handed it to Foley forgetting that the poor jasper couldn't see.

'So what have you gotta say?' Foley's question was animated, his voice energised more than it had been for weeks.

Quickly Reece extracted the document inside. What he found stunned him into silence. He could hardly believe his eyes. Foley could sense the other man's shock at what he was now holding. He let out a gruff chuckle that brought Reece back down to earth.

'H-how in thunderation d-did you get hold of this?' he stuttered, ogling the official contract long since thought to have been destroyed.

'It was tucked away at the back of the safe in Montague's office.' Foley's relaxed levity instantly drained away. 'Once I'd burned my bridges by shooting you down, there was no going back. Getting my hands on the original contract had come too darned late to help either of us. But I thought that maybe sometime in the future it might come in useful.'

Reece responded with a slow nod of agreement.

Foley resumed in a firmer tone of voice. 'Seems like I was right. There's no way I can go back to Three Forks. But you've paid more than enough in blood, sweat and tears for both mine and Abner Montague's skulduggery. Here's the chance for you to see justice meted out in full.'

Reece was breathing hard. 'When I came here, all I wanted was to see you lying in a pool of blood at my feet. Getting revenge had eaten away at my heart for too long. If'n I'd gone through with it, this would never have come to light. It's like a great black cloud has been lifted from my shoulders.'

Foley gingerly held out his hand. 'Does that make us buddies again?'

For an instant, Reece waivered. Then he gripped the proferred appendage.

'I can't never forget, Sam. But I can forgive.'

'That's more than I could ever expect.' Then in a lighter vein, he said, 'Better get Lee Fong out of that cupboard so's he can make us a right dandy supper to celebrate new beginnings. You can stay here the night and head back tomorrow. All I would ask is that you let me know how things go when you confront Montague.'

A dreamy cast suffused Sam Foley's ravaged visage.

'Boy, I'd give anything to see that skunk's face when he realizes his cheating ways have finally been rumbled.'

14

Unforgiven

Reece Willard had left Medicine Hat in something of a daze. He had arrived with every intention of killing his perfidious associate. And it would have been so easy to accomplish the grim deed and disappear back over the border. All that had been thrown into disarray in view of Foley's infirmity, not to mention his obvious remorse.

Then there was the acquisition of the original signed contract that had precipitated the whole sorry episode.

So here he was on the edge of Three Forks wondering how to make the most of this gift from the gods. Various courses of action had been mulled over during the journey south.

He had even considered burning the darned thing and getting on with the rest of his life in the company of the delectable Frenchie La Belle. But that would mean allowing Abner Montague to escape justice, and probably hood-wink other poor suckers, if'n he hadn't already.

No! The bastard was going to pay the full price for his chicanery.

Sam Foley had given him *carte blanche* to draw money on his account in order to secure the services of the finest lawyers. All he needed to do was deliver the document into the hands of a suitable agent along with an account of the whole bizarre story. Then sit back and watch the law take its course.

Firstly, however, he wanted to gloat. To wallow in the varmint's discomfiture when he realized that the game was well and truly up.

Frenchie would be waiting on tenterhooks. He had wired her from Medicine Hat to inform her of the results of his mission. Another half hour wouldn't hurt.

He nudged the horse over to the

hitching rail in front of Montague's Bank. Clutching the vital evidence, he mounted the steps and stepped inside the hallowed portals of the finance house.

All the booths were occupied which satisfied Reece. It enabled him to compose his thoughts. It was important to handle this in a manner that exacted the full panoply of surprise, shock and fear in equal measures.

Peering around, Reece couldn't help but notice a portrait of the conniving bank manager staring down out of a gilt frame. The beady eyes followed him as he walked across the floor. The intention was clearly to intimidate those poor suckers who had fallen behind with their payments.

'You don't scare me, ratface!' he muttered under his breath.

When his turn arrived, Reece asked to see the manager.

'Mr Montague only sees clients with an appointment,' an imperious booby informed the shabby trail bum facing him. The audible sniff was not without substance. Ten days on the trail is apt to make a man's bodily odours rather pungent. 'I trust you have one?'

Reece responded with a rancid smile. But his delivery was brittle and edged with a steel coating.

'He'll want to see me. You tell him that a past acquaintance has information that he will most definitely want to hear. And without delay. Got that, mister? Immediately!' The cogent demand was cemented with a fist hammering down on to the counter. 'Not tomorrow or the next day, but now, pronto. I sure wouldn't want to be in your shoes if'n I have to come back some other time.'

The sheer force of the elocution saw the haughty bank teller hustling over to the door at the rear. He knocked timidly, throwing a nervous glance back towards the tall stranger.

A muffled response found him gingerly entering the inner sanctum.

Minutes passed. Then the teller

emerged and gestured for Reece to come round the side of the booths into the bank's working area. He held the door open. The newcomer held his breath, pulling the brim of his hat down to conceal his features.

The door closed with a soft plop.

Not wishing to show undue curiosity regarding this unusual request for an interview, the manager busied himself with some papers on his desk. He did not look up, forcing the newcomer to stand waiting on the far side of the large desk. It was a ploy meant to convey who was holding the reins of power.

Reece was unphased by the varmint's odious tactics. If necessary, he would wait all day. The result would be the same.

Abner Montague was finished. His reputation trampled into the dust. Once the truth was made public, he would become a heinous pariah that folks would avoid like the plague. His days of cheating innocent people were over.

The next step was a court case and, if justice were to be served, a long term in the state penitentiary.

Five minutes passed before the manager laid down his pen and looked up. The potential client's face was wreathed in shadow.

'My clerk tells me that you have some vital information,' he snorted. 'I am a busy man. So if you could reveal the nature of this supposed announcement, perhaps I could judge for myself.'

With deliberate slowness, Reece extracted the document from the envelope and held it up at arms length. He had no intention of allowing the crooked varmint to get his hands on it. The official nature of the ornately drawn-up contract with its red seal and signatures was clearly evident.

Montague frowned. His thick eyebrows met in the middle. Grasping hands reached out. But the document was quickly pulled back.

'What is this?' he snapped. 'Some kind of joke?'

'It's no joke, Montague,' hissed the newcomer. 'And I sure ain't laughing. Not yet anyway. But I will be when you've been put behind bars.'

'How dare you come in here threatening me,' exclaimed the irate banker jumping to his feet. 'Get out before I call the sheriff.'

Reece tilted the broad-brimmed hat up to reveal his face.

'You again,' Montague croaked. His face assumed a waxy palor. His mouth dropped open. Again his terrified eyes focused on the document.

'Sit down!'

The icy rasp was like a punch in the guts, forcing the banker to slump back into his seat.

'Guess you must know what this is,' Reece smirked. 'Just to refresh your memory. It's the original and genuine contract that you changed. And by doing that you sentenced me to seven years of hell in the pen by forcing me and Sam Foley to break the law.'

'B-but it can't be,' stammered the

panic-stricken banker. 'I . . . I . . . '

'You reckoned that it had been destroyed,' Reece finished the stuttering assumption. 'Well, by some stroke of luck for me, you must have overlooked it. My partner found it in the safe after he shot me and robbed the safe. He couldn't do nothing about it. But I have served my time. So there is nothing to stop me from turning this over to a lawyer and having you indicted for fraud.' Reece waved the piece of parchment in the banker's face. 'And sure as eggs is eggs, I'm not the only one you've cheated over the years. Once this comes out, others are sure to come forward.'

Emitting a harsh laugh, Reece swung on his heels and made to leave.

'See you in court, mister,' he scoffed.

At that very moment there was a knock on the door and a small prim woman entered the room.

Without preamble, she announced in a breathless hurry, 'I'm sorry to interrupt, sir. But Mr Crosby from head office has arrived for a spot check on the books. I thought you would want to know . . . '

That was as far as she got. A piercing scream rent the tense atmosphere.

Immediately that Reece had turned his back, Montague knew that his whole life was in the balance. The arrival of the bank's chief auditor was the last straw. He had hoped for a week at least to doctor the accounts in his favour. That was now impossible. In a split second, all these thoughts flashed through Abner Montague's tortured brain.

Panic gripped his innards. Without thinking he reached down to a drawer in his desk and removed a Colt Lightning revolver. The small gun spat lead just as the secretary was making her announcement.

Reece's reaction was instant.

He threw himself to one side, bundling the unfortunate female beneath him. The glass door shattered into myriad fragments. Another shot rang out. The bullet singed Reece's left arm, a searing jolt that drew blood. Again the unfortunate secretary screamed out in terror.

Reece rolled away, extracting his own revolver as yet another slug chewed at the floorboards inches from his head. But his own gun was already offering a lethal response. Three shots in rapid succession found their mark. Even under such an intense attack, Reece Willard attempted to place his shots in non life-threatening positions. Killing the skunk would be too quick.

The Lightning fell from Montague's shattered hand. He fell back, blood pouring from the other wounds.

Out in the main body of the bank, chaos was rampant as customers and employees sought cover. One enterprising individual must have had the acumen to escape. Within minutes, the brusquely officious voice of Sheriff Mort Harding pierced the general cacophony.

'Throw your gun out the door,' he called. 'The bank is surrounded. You can't escape so come out with hands raised.'

Reece was taking no chances of being shot down. His gun landed with a clatter on the floorboards of the front office.

'I'm coming out, Sheriff,' he shouted back, 'and I've got a young lady with me who has just saved my life.'

'That's true, Sheriff,' the secretary chirped up, her cracked voice harsh and strident from the traumatic experience. 'Mr Montague was about to shoot this man in the back when I came in.'

'And you better send for a sawbones,' Reece added. 'Montague is bleeding like a sieve.'

'You first, Miss Fenchurch,' replied Harding, signalling for a bystander to fetch the doctor.

After the shaken secretary had emerged it was Reece's turn.

'You have some explaining to do, Willard,' rapped the lawman when he recognized the emerging gunslick. He made certain that his own shooter was rock steady. 'And it better be good.'

Two hours later, Reece was upstairs in the private quarters of Frenchie La Belle. He had been confident of being able to explain the brutal events at the bank, thanks to the welcome testimony of Miss Amelia Fenchurch.

After being released, he had sought out a reputable lawyer in town and appraised him of the whole situation. The all-important loan agreement had been lodged in the attorney's safe. The man had assured him that with this irrefutable evidence, the outcome of Montague's trial for attempted murder and fraud was a foregone conclusion. He would be going down for a hefty spell. And that was in addition to suspicions harboured by the bank's representative regarding their manager's cooking of the books.

Reece flopped down on the sofa. He was plum tuckered out.

'I could sleep for a week,' came the slurred remark as he sipped at the glass of champagne. His eyes drooped as total exhaustion threatened to envelop his shattered frame.

Much as Frenchie was anxious to learn about his encounter with Sam Foley, she knew that rest was a first priority.

However . . .

'Not before you kiss me,' she purred in his ear. 'And tell me that we'll never be parted, ever again.'

A single eye opened. The ardent gleam matched a crafty smirk.

Carefully, he placed the glass on a table and took her in his arms. Their lips met. A melding of hearts fused in passion. Finally they broke apart.

'Does that answer your query, Mrs Willard?'

THE END

We do hope that you have enjoyed reading this large print book.

Did you know that all of our titles are available for purchase?

We publish a wide range of high quality large print books including:
**Romances, Mysteries, Classics
General Fiction
Non Fiction and Westerns**

Special interest titles available in large print are:
**The Little Oxford Dictionary
Music Book, Song Book
Hymn Book, Service Book**

Also available from us courtesy of Oxford University Press:
**Young Readers' Dictionary
(large print edition)
Young Readers' Thesaurus
(large print edition)**

For further information or a free brochure, please contact us at:
**Ulverscroft Large Print Books Ltd.,
The Green, Bradgate Road, Anstey,
Leicester, LE7 7FU, England.
Tel:** (00 44) **0116 236 4325
Fax:** (00 44) **0116 234 0205**

Sandy Rivers and two fellow trail hands were taking a well-deserved rest in the Durant saloon when the injured man staggered to their table — whipped half to death, then knifed in the back. He had come to warn them of something — but died before he could finish what he had to say . . . The knife and lash-marks appear to implicate their old trail boss Amos Coyne; when he then steals the hands' horses, stranding all three men in Durant, there's nothing for it but to se out and track him down . . .